Yuled BY THE ORCS

A HOLIDAY MONSTER ROMANCE TALE

FINLEY FENN

Editing: Eris Adderly
Cover artwork: Skadior Art
Cover design update: Sylvia Frost at The Book Brander
Typography and original cover design: Finley Fenn
Supported by the generous members of the Orc Sworn Patreon

~

Yuled by the Orcs

~

Sign up at www.finleyfenn.com for bonus stories and epilogues, delicious orc artwork, complete content guidance, news about upcoming books, and more!

ALSO BY FINLEY FENN

ORC SWORN

The Lady and the Orc

The Heiress and the Orc

The Librarian and the Orc

The Duchess and the Orc

The Midwife and the Orc

The Maid and the Orcs

The Governess and the Orc

The Beauty and the Orcs

The Widow and the Orcs

The Artist and the Orc

The Ex and the Orcs

Offered by the Orc

Tryggred by the Orc

Yuled by the Orcs

Tales of Orc Sworn

ORC FORGED

The Sins of the Orc

The Fall of the Orc

THE MAGES

The Mage's Maid

The Mage's Match

The Mage's Master

The Mage's Groom

To my extremely generous supporters on Patreon! Thank you and Happy Yule!

1

It was the night before Yule, and Lydia was off to meet an orc.

She drew in a deep, fortifying breath of the crisp cool air as she walked, her boots crunching in the light snow beneath her feet. It was a clear, quiet night, and the forest seemed to glitter in the bright moonlight from above, sparkling white and silver. Whispering of peace and calm and ease, in utter contradiction to the ever-rising hammer of Lydia's heartbeat.

She was going to meet an orc. For Yule. Alone.

And gods, it still felt impossibly unreal. For a shy, awkward, widowed washerwoman to be rushing off into the night, meeting in secret with an orc. An orc who had to be a good decade older than her own forty-odd years, his tall rangy body covered with battle scars, his hair and beard gone fully silver.

And his name was *Sigtryggr*, of all things. Sigtryggr, of Clan Skai.

"Call me Tryg, for short," he'd informed Lydia when he'd first appeared in her tiny kitchen, flashing her a wry, sharp-toothed grin. "Sigtryggr's too much of a mouthful for even my own kin to bear, ach?"

Lydia had been desperately attempting to stave off the forthcoming fainting spell—there was an orc, in her *house*—and even more alarming, said orc was eyeing her with keen, glinting interest. His gaze holding first on her grey-streaked brown hair, and then her round, perpetually flushed cheeks, before sliding down to her soft, plump body beneath her shabby work dress.

Lydia had frozen under the scrutiny, because it had been so, so long since someone had looked at her like that. Since her husband Tom's passing, perhaps, a good decade before. And yes, in the years after, there'd been a few men from the village sniffing about, but once they'd learned that she was unable to have children, they'd almost instantly scurried off again. And ever since, she'd just kept her head down, just doing her work, living her quiet, dull little life, like the unin-teresting, uninspiring washerwoman she was.

And clearly the orc had also realized his mistake, because he'd abruptly swung a heavy sack off his shoulder, and plunked it onto the middle of Lydia's washing table. "I'm told you're the best woman to ask about laundry, in these parts," he'd said, raising an angular silver eyebrow toward her. "An' that you'll get it done quick, with no fuss."

Right. *Laundry.* So Lydia had gulped down a choked breath of air, and reached to open the sack with shaky hands. Indeed finding it full of ordinary-looking tunics and trousers, and a few strangely sweet-smelling bedlinens, as well.

"Erm, um, yes," she'd somehow sputtered, though her hands had still been trembling. "You—your usual washer isn't on hand anymore?"

At that, the orc—*Tryg*, he'd said—had chuckled, the

sound deep and disarmingly warm. "Well, there's been a bit of fuss over the laundry, back home," he'd replied, "and m'boy Tryggr's been dragged into helping out. Don't want to add his old Pa's dirty washing into his pile too, you ken?"

It had taken Lydia a long, halting moment to digest all that—first, the surprising fact that an *orc* would have such consideration toward his son's workload, and secondly, the fact that said orc had apparently given his son nearly the same bizarre name as the one he himself possessed. And third, the way the laundry's sweet scent had begun coiling strange and deep in her belly, twisting together in highly unnerving ways with this Tryg's warm, patient smile.

"So you'll take it, then?" he'd said, his voice dropping a shade lower than before. "I'll pay double. An' in advance. If that helps."

Well. That was no small offer, and Lydia had finally, shakily nodded, and taken his proffered coins. And then she'd spent all the next day frantically washing, airing, and pressing his clothes, breathing in their sweet scent, all while glancing again and again over her shoulder toward the door.

And when Tryg had reappeared at the door, two days later, there'd been an odd, excited-feeling leap in Lydia's belly. Especially when he'd exclaimed with all apparent delight over his sack of neatly folded laundry, and then flashed her a stunning, sharp-toothed grin.

"That's good, sweet thing," he'd told her, his black eyes glinting warm and approving. "Real good. Thank you."

Lydia had flushed Yund waved it away, though she hadn't seemed able to pull her eyes from his angular, bearded face. From the way his silver head was slowly tilting, as a long, sinuous black tongue briefly brushed against his lips.

"Don't s'pose," he'd said, his voice all soft liquid heat, "there's anything else I could offer you, as thanks?"

Lydia's heart had been racing again, her own tongue brushing her lips. And when Tryg had stepped closer, and slowly slipped his clawed hand against her waist, she'd shuddered all over, and met his warm, patient eyes. Eyes that had twinkled with easy indulgence as he'd drawn her even closer, and bent his head into her neck.

It had somehow ended with Lydia on her back on the washing table, while Tryg had knelt on the floor before her, feasting with shameless, shocking abandon between her legs. Hurling her full of stunning, staggering pleasure, unlike anything she'd felt in years. Decades. Pleasure that felt far too vivid, too powerful, to be real.

And afterwards, Tryg hadn't made demands, or even requested any sort of reciprocation. Instead, he'd stood up, straightened out Lydia's rumpled dress, and slung his sack of clean laundry over his shoulder.

"Thanks again, sweet thing," he'd said, with a wink, and another one of those grins. "Mayhap I'll bring by more laundry next week, ach?"

Lydia had been left entirely unable to speak, but she'd somehow managed a curt, desperate nod. And when Tryg had indeed returned the next week, they'd done it again, and then again. And if her efforts at pleasing him in return had been awkward at first, or fumbling, or inexperienced, he hadn't at all complained. And instead, he'd only kept blatantly demonstrating what he liked, rewarding her eager attempts with praise and affection and pleasure.

But afterwards, he would invariably throw that sack over his shoulder, and stride out again. Leaving Lydia staring silent and forlorn after him, alone in the empty, echoing kitchen. Until she'd begun to feel almost sick with hunger and longing, with the strange, steadily rising urge to ask him to stay. To beg him to hold her close and safe, deep into the night. To plead for promises that he surely had no interest whatsoever in making, let alone keeping.

"Have you ever been married?" she'd blurted out one day, as Tryg had turned to leave again. "Or... attached, somehow, to a woman?"

It had been a reasonable question, she'd thought, especially given his obvious fondness for his son, who he often mentioned—but he'd actually chuckled as he'd turned around again, giving a regretful shake of his head.

"Ach, no," he'd replied, with a crooked little smile. "I've always loved you women, with your sweet scents and squeals—but you're always far too jealous, ach? Never know how to share, you ken. An' even if you claim you do"—his lips had thinned, his eyes angling away, as if with some bitter memory—"you yet rage and weep when you hear you ain't the only one. Let alone *witnessing* it."

Oh. Ohhhh. Tryg had—*other lovers*. Lydia's stomach had horribly plummeted, her mouth quivering, because—oh. She was just—a side activity for him. A diversion, perhaps. And truly, what else had she expected? She was a plain, poor, boring washerwoman, with a wrinkled brow, a flushed face, and perpetually red, chapped hands. Of course this hadn't meant anything to him. Of *course*.

And damn it, Tryg had been studying her with close, watchful attention, his eyes narrowing. "Wish me to stop coming, then, woman?" he'd asked, very smoothly. "You not willing to share either? Not even in this?"

But Lydia had swallowed hard, and rubbed at her hot face, and fought through the bitter swelling misery. No. He couldn't stop coming. Not when he was quite possibly the best thing that had ever happened in her quiet, empty life. *No.*

"Please, don't stop coming," she'd told him, her voice

cracking. "*Please.* To be frank, I'll likely go along with anything you please—anything you want from me—as long as you keep coming."

Tryg had eyed her for a long moment, but he'd bent down and kissed her with surprising gentleness before saying farewell. And then he'd indeed kept coming, without fail, week after week. Until summer had slowly slipped into fall, and then the cold, dark nights of winter.

But he still hadn't once attempted to stay the night, or to take things any further than their shared pleasures together. And Lydia hadn't once asked, either, or brought up his other lovers again. Until a day several weeks before, when Tryg had slung his sack over his shoulder, turning as usual toward the door—but then, without warning, he'd spun to face her again.

"Like to spend Yule with me, woman?" he'd said. "I could get us a little lodge nearby to cozy up in for a few nights. Not my home, you ken, but a place my clan keeps for aught such as this."

Oh. Lydia's brows had shot up, her eyes searching his face, because there'd been something—different, there. Something she couldn't at all read. But she'd still fervently, frantically nodded, her heart leaping in her chest, because he wanted to spend Yule with her. *Yule.* For a *few nights.*

"I'd love to, thank you," she'd told him, with a swift, genuine smile. "When? Where? And what can I bring? Is there anything you'd like for a gift?"

Perhaps it had been far too eager, because Tryg had glanced away again, rubbing at the back of his neck. "Ach, no gifts," he'd said flatly. "Mayhap you can wear a pretty frock, or some such, should you wish. But no more."

Lydia had instantly agreed, and hadn't been able to resist giving him an impulsive hug, which he'd returned with an indulgent pat to her head. And then she'd begun making arrangements, and counting down the slow, endless days until Yule.

And now, Yule's Eve had finally arrived. And Lydia had waited until dark, and then closed up her little cottage on the outskirts of the village, and crept into the moonlit forest. Carefully following the directions Tryg had given her, her heartbeat rising with every step. Follow the road to the river, and then turn left, and cross the log bridge. And then keep going south, until... until...

There. A thin wisp of grey smoke, streaking up into the night sky. And Lydia's steps quickened as she strode toward it, toward where she could indeed see a cozy little stone cottage, tucked into the surrounding snow-capped trees.

She halted at the wooden front door, dragging in long, deep breaths. Fighting to calm her frantic, furious heartbeat as she slowly raised her hand to knock...

But then, without warning, the door swung open. And there, standing tall behind it, was a powerful, grey-skinned, silver-bearded orc. An orc with sharp teeth, pointed ears, and a broad, stunning smile.

"Finally, sweet thing," Tryg said. "Come in."

2

Lydia followed Tryg into the cottage with shy, tentative steps, her eyes sweeping around the little room.

It was surprisingly warm and snug, with a merry fire crackling in the fireplace, and a few simple, sturdy wood furnishings scattered throughout. A table and chairs, a shelf holding a few carved figures, and a large, fur-covered bed. And perched atop the fireplace mantel, there were multiple boughs of fresh-cut spruce and fir, their scent filling the air with warmth and sweetness.

But most compelling of all, of course, was Tryg himself. Standing tall and rangy and bare-chested before her, his beard neatly trimmed, his silver hair pulled up into a messy knot, stabbed through with a gleaming, deadly-looking dagger. And as always, his grin was impossibly contagious, showing all his sharp white teeth, and deeply crinkling the corners of his glittering black eyes.

"Ach, I've missed you, sweet thing," he purred, as he stepped close, and tilted up Lydia's face with an easy, familiar clawed hand. "Look how flushed and pretty you are. Were you eager to see me, too?"

Lydia's cheeks heated as she nodded, and Tryg's grin broadened even further, his eyes dancing in the firelight. "Good," he said. "Now, I've gained us a nice festive supper, should you wish? And I snatched some treats from home, too."

Tryg's home, Lydia now knew, was Orc Mountain, the terrifyingly large fortress that loomed a day's journey to the south, and teemed with hordes of raging, ravenous orcs—or so the tales went. But as Tryg carefully took off Lydia's cloak, and hung it on a nearby hook, she once again found herself utterly unable to reconcile all the horrifying stories of Orc Mountain with the reality of this particular orc. With the way he'd turned to grin at her again, his eyes lingering with frank appreciation on the thin, form-fitting red dress she'd worn beneath her cloak.

"You gain this frock just for me, sweet pet?" he asked, with a blatant curl of his black tongue against his lips. "Very pretty. I like."

The relief swarmed up Lydia's spine, and in that instant, all the trouble she'd gone through for this dress—travelling out of town, haggling with the tailor, spending the greater part of Tryg's exceedingly generous payments upon it—felt entirely worthwhile. Especially as he kept looking at her like that, like she was the only bedmate in his world, like there was no one else...

"Come," he said, with another stunning grin, as he nudged her toward the table. "Sit. Drink. Eat."

Only now did Lydia notice the two chipped, steaming mugs on the table, and the overflowing tray of fresh-looking sweets and pastries. And once she'd gone and sat down,

Tryg strode over to the fireplace, and brought back two bowls of succulent-smelling stew, too.

"This is delicious," Lydia told him, with genuine surprise, after she'd carefully tasted a spoonful. "I didn't realize you could cook."

She belatedly winced at the implied insult in the words, but across the table, Tryg laughed and waved it away before loading up his own spoon. "Ach, you don't want to eat my cooking, pet," he said cheerfully. "But m'boy, he's made some good friends in the kitchen back home, so he's got me sorted."

Tryg's smile had gone soft and fond, the way it always did when he spoke of his son, and Lydia couldn't deny the pang in her chest as she smiled back toward him. "You don't mind being parted from him for Yule?" she asked, tentative. "Isn't it time you'd usually spend together?"

Tryg waved it away again, and then reached for a cake, snapping it in two with his sharp teeth. "Ach, m'boy's got a sweet new mate to dote upon, these days," he said lightly. "But he said he might bring him out later, if you'd wish to meet 'em."

Oh. Lydia's spoon froze halfway to her mouth, because had he—had he just said that his son's mate was another *male*? Another *orc*, surely? And far more importantly, Tryg wanted—he wanted Lydia to *meet* them?!

"Ach, no need to scent so vexed, woman," Tryg said now, more clipped than before. "Don't need to meet 'em, if you don't wish. If you're one of those humans who don't approve of males finding joy together."

There was a flinty glint in his eyes as he spoke, and Lydia felt herself blanching, her head shaking. "I do want to meet them," she said firmly. "Very much. I'm only—surprised. That you would... want me to."

She couldn't hide the uncertainty in her voice, but across from her Tryg cocked his head, his eyes intent. "Why wouldn't I wish you to meet 'em?" he said. "We've shared much joy together, these past moons. M'boy's oft asked after your scent upon me."

Right. Lydia's face was heating again, but she jerked a shrug, and drew in a shaky breath. "I just know you have... others, in your life," she said thickly. "Others who are... probably much more important to you."

There was an instant's dangling silence, and across the table, Tryg's face had gone entirely blank—and too late, Lydia flapped her reddened hand at him, and then cringed and shoved it under the table. "Which is *fine*," she blurted out. "I understand, of course. I'm sure your other lovers are younger, and wealthier, and better looking, and probably have far more experience pleasing you, and—"

Her voice abruptly broke off, because Tryg's long arm had snapped across the table, his hand clasping her shoulder. "Enough of that, pet," he said, gentle but firm. "I don't care for any of that. You live this life as long as I have, you learn what holds true weight, ach? A kind heart and an eager touch hold far more worth than all these fleeting fripperies."

Oh. Lydia bit her lip, blinking back toward him, and he flashed her a crooked, affectionate smile. "But you are yet stunning, pet," he said, even softer. "Your scent, and your pretty eyes, and your sweet little womb, and the hunger in your touch—*ach*. Why do you ken I cannot keep myself away, human as you are? When even now, I wonder whether you spoke truth, when you said you should welcome—"

He stopped there, his mouth twisting, but Lydia could easily follow the rest of it. He was talking about... the *sharing* again. And about her promise that she didn't mind. *You yet rage and weep when you hear you're not the only one.*

Lydia couldn't seem to find a response to that, and Tryg's eyes were studying her again, glinting with a strange, shimmering intensity. "But... you swore this sharing would not vex you," he continued, quiet. "Do you"—he hesitated, tilted his head—"do you yet mean this? Enough to prove this to me?"

Lydia swallowed hard, her heartbeat lurching—what did he mean by *proving* it?—but then she felt herself exhale, heavy but certain. "Y-yes," she said, her voice only slightly wavering. "I would try to do whatever I could to prove it to you. I"—she drew in air, courage—"I like you a lot, Tryg. So much. And"—she swallowed again, held his eyes—"I... I trust you."

It was an inexplicable sentiment, and no doubt an unaccountably foolish one, because Tryg had made Lydia no promises, hadn't even stayed a single night. But as she looked at those glinting eyes across the table, her words still felt deeply, damnably true. She did trust him. He wouldn't hurt her, or mock her, or abandon her without warning. He wouldn't.

Tryg gazed back at her for another long moment, his shoulders rising and falling, but then he gave a quick, decisive little nod. "Ach, then, sweet thing," he said firmly. "Finish that, and then I've got a gift for you."

A gift? Lydia blinked toward him, but his eyes had shuttered again, his hand waving purposefully at the stew and treats. So she readily obliged, even as a low, whispering unease kept rising in her chest. He'd brought her a gift, after he'd so roundly refused one from her? And this gift... did it have anything to do with the question he'd asked just before it?

Do you yet mean this? Enough to prove this to me?

But Tryg didn't speak again, seeming fully focused on the delicious meal, so Lydia attempted to do the same. It truly was wonderful, between the rich stew, the flaky pastries, and the hot mulled cider. And combined with the cozy room, and the crackling fire, and the sweet scent of the spruce and fir, her unease seemed to catch and tangle with a deep, powerful longing. Gods, if only this could truly be hers. If only he could truly be hers.

And as she finished eating, it occurred to her that Tryg was looking uneasy, too. His black claws drumming on the table, his eyes darting repeatedly toward the door. Until he finally shoved back his chair and leapt to his feet, pacing toward the door, and then whirling around toward Lydia again.

"Are you ready?" he demanded. "For your gift?"

Lydia's heart again kicked in her chest, but she drew in another shaky breath, and nodded, and stood. And watched, unblinking, as Tryg strode to the door, and swung it open. And behind it was...

Another *orc*.

3

The orc in the door was terrifying.

He was huge, greenish-grey, and utterly hideous, with a ruined nose, a split lip, and a heavy, horribly scarred face, framed by thick, long black hair. His pointed ears were puffy and bulbous, his eyelids were mottled black, and when he pulled back his lips—perhaps in a smile—Lydia could see that one of his fangs was broken off, his other teeth jagged and crooked in his mouth.

Lydia's hands clapped over her own mouth, her eyes wide and arrested on the orc's appalling face. While Tryg—Tryg was reaching for the orc, and...

Hugging him. Yes, *hugging* him, yanking him into a tight, close embrace. His hand slapping again and again to the orc's massive shoulder, his head ducking brief but meaningful into that scarred, corded neck.

"Hullo, sweet *elskan*," Tryg said, muffled against the orc's skin. "Thank you for coming, ach?"

The hideous new orc's mouth was still pulled into

something that must have been a smile, and his eyes fluttered closed, his big scarred hand gripping just as tightly at Tryg's back. The touch easy, familiar... and *intimate*.

But it was only for a moment, because the ugly orc was already pulling away from Tryg, and straightening out his cloak as he turned toward... *Lydia*. And then he gave her a deep, fluid-looking bow, his huge fist pressed against his heart.

"Greetings, woman," he said, in a surprisingly low, soft voice. "I have heard so much of you, these past moons."

Oh. Lydia's clammy-feeling hands had still been clapped to her mouth, but she guiltily shoved them downwards, and gulped for breath. "Th-thank you," she choked. "I'm—Lydia. A—washerwoman. Tryg's—friend."

She thrust out her chapped, red hand toward the new orc, wincing at the sight of it trembling between them—but the orc gently took it in his own, clasping it with warm, careful pressure. And then—Lydia blanched—he bent over it, and brought it to his mouth. *Kissing* it, oh gods, the touch of his lips light and soft, his breath hot against her skin.

Lydia stood watching, frozen, not breathing—and when the orc finally stood tall again, her hand was still clasped in his, and he was still smiling. Or at least, she was quite certain it was a smile now, judging by that deep crinkle at the corners of his eyes.

"I am Ezog, of Clan Bautul," the orc told her, again in that smooth, velvety voice. "But you may call me whatever best pleases you."

Lydia shivered, her hand twitching in his, but the orc—*Ezog*—didn't pull away, and for some inexplicable reason, she didn't, either. Though her uncertain gaze had flicked toward Tryg, who was beaming back and forth between them, his eyes bright with satisfaction. And then he reached toward Ezog again, this time to pull the cloak from his broad shoulders.

And—wait. Beneath the cloak, this Ezog was... *unclothed.* Unclothed, his huge body fully naked, except for... for...

A single wide, shining red ribbon. Around his...

Lydia's entire body shocked to stillness, her disbelieving eyes gaping at the sight of it. He was wearing a ribbon. Only a ribbon. On his bare... *cock.*

She stared at it for another long, swinging, staggering moment—and then, without at all meaning to, she glanced up and down the rest of his bare, massive, muscular form. The skin was the same deep greenish grey as his face, and it was patterned all over with more vivid, awful scars. Some looking truly gruesome, like the huge gouge in his hip, or the large, blotchy discolouration over his knee. And in truth, the only place that had been spared the scarring was... *that.* That long, plump, soft-looking cock, dangling at his groin, with that incongruous red ribbon tied around it.

Impossible. *Unthinkable.* And Lydia was again staring toward it, and then darting another wide, panicked look up at Tryg's face. Because oh gods, what was this, what must he think of this, and—

And wait. *Wait.* Tryg was—smiling. Smiling with warm, unmistakable fondness toward this Ezog. And then—Lydia's breath choked—he blatantly reached down a clawed hand, and gave that dangling beribboned cock a gentle, familiar-looking squeeze.

"Very pretty, *elskan,*" he murmured, with a flick of his claw at the red silk ribbon. "I like."

Oh. It was the exact same thing he'd said to Lydia about her red dress, and she still couldn't seem to move, her stomach plummeting in her belly. And suddenly, both orcs turned toward her, Ezog's brow deeply furrowing, Tryg's gone carefully blank.

"Ach, woman," he said, his voice very smooth. "Ezog is my gift to you, this Yule's Eve. Shall you accept him from me?"

4

E zog was her *gift*? For *Yule*?!

Lydia felt like she'd been spun upside-down, suddenly, like the world had swept away into some kind of bizarre, baffling dream. Tryg was giving her another entire *orc*? As a gift?!

And it was... *this* orc?! The most hideously terrifying creature she'd ever seen in her dull, quiet little life?

But both orcs were both still looking intently toward her, Tryg with that chilly distance in his usually warm eyes, and Ezog with genuine-looking concern. And as Lydia gaped back and forth between them, it occurred to her that this was perhaps... a test.

Do you yet mean this? Enough to prove this to me?

And she'd said... *Yes. I would try to do whatever I could to prove it to you. I... trust you.*

And this—*this*, here, now, was clearly what Tryg wanted. He was clearly very familiar with this Ezog—because this Ezog was obviously one of his other *lovers*, gods damn it. And Tryg wanted to see if Lydia truly wanted it, too. If she'd truly meant it.

You're always far too jealous, ach? Never know how to share.

And—well. If it was a choice between Tryg and—well. And gods, if he would just stop looking at her like that, as if Lydia was failing him even in her hesitation, just as he'd perhaps expected, or dreaded, or even feared.

"That is—very generous," she finally croaked, her voice not at all her own. "Of—both of you. But I don't—I'm not at all sure how a gift like this works, exactly?"

Her voice sounded high-pitched, utterly unrecognizable—but oh, it had been entirely worth it, because the grin had leapt back to Tryg's mouth, so sudden and stunning she nearly swayed on her feet.

"Ach, I see, sweet thing," he said, as he reached his big hand to clasp her shoulder, drawing her a little closer. "When a Skai offers you a gift thus, it's meant only to gain your pleasure for a spell, ach? No need to swear vows, or make promises, or aught of that sort."

Oh. A distant relief swarmed in Lydia's chest, but she could scarcely manage a nod, especially when Tryg again grinned at Ezog, with palpable affection sparkling in his eyes. "But should you accept, woman," he continued, "my *elskan* will join us this Yule, and until we part, he'll be here to serve your whims. To pet you all over, or make you scream upon his tongue, or aught else you might wish."

Oh. Right. So this was... the *sharing*, then. This was what Tryg had been speaking of. Although—Lydia found herself frowning toward him, her head tilting—surely when he'd spoken of sharing, he'd meant for *his* pleasure, too? It was *him* who had the other lovers, right? *He* was the one who clearly cared for this Ezog?

"But—what about you?" she stammered at him. "What about your pleasure?"

Tryg blinked at her, once—but then his smile seemed to

flash even brighter, his arm reaching to slip around her shoulders. "You are so sweet, my pretty pet," he purred. "But you ken, I shall take great joy from this, ach? I shall revel in showing my *elskan* your fair form this Yule, and teaching him how pretty you are when you squeal upon my strong Skai prick, and drink up my good Skai seed. And to do all this, whilst he also tends you and cares for you and draws out your hunger—*ach*. This shall make our joy all the sweeter, you ken?"

Oh. The air had entirely vanished from Lydia's lungs, and her eyes darted again toward this Ezog, who was—somehow—still holding her hand with warm, gentle pressure. "I shall do naught you do not wish for, woman," he said in his low, velvety voice, at such strange, surreal odds with his scarred, ruined face. "I am only here to serve, and help build upon the joy Tryg brings you."

It was taking another moment for Lydia to digest all this—they meant Ezog's... *attentions...* would be *supplemental* to Tryg's, then? And Tryg was indeed flashing her another bright, encouraging smile, and drawing her even closer into his side.

"Ach, just like that," he said. "Only what pleases you, my sweet, even if that's only his touch. But I'd be remiss not to tell you he's got a wicked tongue, and you'd regret wasting it."

With that, Tryg actually winked down toward Lydia, as if seeing Ezog using his *tongue* on her would truly be something he would enjoy. And wait, did he mean—was he saying *he'd* experienced Ezog's tongue, too?

But yes, yes, of course he had. Ezog was one of Tryg's lovers, and now he wanted to... share. As a gift. For Lydia's... *joy.*

And as she blinked back and forth between them, it

distantly occurred to her that she had nothing to lose in trying it. This was obviously important to Tryg. This was something he wanted from the lovers in his life. And if she walked out now, she would surely lose him anyway, so why not make the attempt? Why not... just see where it went, and then make a choice?

So Lydia braced herself, and met Tryg's eyes, and perhaps even squeezed Ezog's warm hand. A test. A gift.

"Thank you for such a generous Yule gift, Tryg," she said, as steadily as she could. "I'm honoured to accept."

5

Lydia's words were met by yet another broad, delighted grin from Tryg, and a gentle, approving squeeze of Ezog's hand against hers.

"You honour us also, sweet thing," Tryg said, as he bent down, and pressed a soft kiss to Lydia's hair. "I'll be most glad to share this with you, this Yule."

Oh. Lydia felt her face deeply flushing, tilting into the familiar, sweet-scented warmth of Tryg's neck, and he drew her even closer into his side, his big hand slipping up and down her back with smooth, steady reassurance. "Now, to begin," he purred, "I ken you oughta be shown your new gift, ach?"

She should? Lydia was again glancing uncertainly toward Ezog, who was already very much on display, especially with that incongruous red bow still tied around his plump green shaft. But Tryg was nudging her a little forward, and even giving an encouraging slap to her arse.

"Gotta unwrap him, sweet thing," he said lightly. "Then take a good look, ach? See what you might like to make full use of, these next days."

Lydia's shock surged once again—she really would be *making use* of such a horrifyingly hideous orc? But she managed a shaky nod, and jerked a step forward. Toward— her gift. Who she was supposed to... *unwrap.*

Her hand was still clasped in Ezog's warm, steady grip, and at least that seemed to make it easier, somehow. Easier, good gods, to drop her blinking eyes back to that thick, silken red ribbon, tied around that long, bulky cock.

It was still soft, she realized, with yet another jolt of shock, because it already was quite... improbably propor- tioned. And yes, Tryg himself had also been a surprise in that regard—but Tryg's was slimmer and paler, almost always rigid and ready, and latticed all over with veins and multiple scars. While this—this fat, smooth, soft-looking length—felt entirely different, somehow. As if it wasn't made to jab inside and make one scream, but to softly open one around it, and then lock itself deep into place.

But Lydia still couldn't seem to move any further, let alone reach out toward it—and she was distantly, deeply grateful when Ezog himself guided her hand closer. Giving her fingers another gentle squeeze before releasing them, so close, now only a breath away...

And it almost felt like someone else, looked like someone else, as Lydia's familiar, trembling fingers reached out to the edge of that red ribbon, and grasped it. And then pulled, drawing the ribbon away, away, away, until it was dangling loose in her hand. While the cock she'd unwrapped was no longer dangling at all, but visibly flexing and swelling. Rising.

Lydia's throat convulsed as she watched, as that deep green flesh shuddered, expanded, lengthened. Growing fatter and longer with every breath, until it had become something truly, impossibly obscene. Something that couldn't actually be real, except that it was, it *was*—and beside her Tryg was merrily chuckling, and again giving a reassuring pat to her back.

"Again, no need to take it inside you, should you not wish," he purred at her. "But it's so pretty, is it not? Should you not wish to touch it, at least?"

Oh. Lydia's throat convulsed again, her eyes darting up toward Tryg's smug face, and then to Ezog's. To where, yes, he was still just as hideous as before, but somehow the truth of that seemed a little more blunted than it had previously. Especially with how he was again smiling at her, his eyes crinkling at the corners.

"Only should you wish," he told her, in that quiet, reassuring voice. "I am here to serve."

But Lydia couldn't stop searching his soft, strangely expressive eyes, while a new, unnerving uncertainty coiled in her belly. "But—you're *sure* you really want this?" she whispered. "Truly?"

Ezog's nod was slow but certain, and yes, that was definitely another smile, crinkling even deeper on his eyes. "Ach, yes," he replied, his voice low and fervent. "To gain the touch and the scent and the joy of such a sweet, pretty woman—this is a great gift to me, also."

Oh. Lydia glanced toward Tryg again, but he was looking back at Ezog, his eyes unmistakably fond. As if... as if this entire bizarre scenario had been meant as a gift for *Ezog*, too. For Tryg's other lover. For someone he obviously deeply cared about.

So Lydia drew in a breath, gave a furtive nod. And then, she slowly, slowly moved her hand closer, until... she touched it. *Touched* Ezog, there, on that massive, jutting green length. Feeling the impossible softness of that warm skin, and how the strength beneath shuddered and swelled even fuller against her light, tentative touch.

"Ach, that's it," came Tryg's husky voice, close in her ear. "Take a good long look, sweet thing. Get to know what's yours."

Something hitched deep in Lydia's groin, because she knew that voice of Tryg's—and yes, yes, that was the familiar hunger, flashing in his eyes as he watched. Saying, all too plainly, that he liked watching this. Liked seeing her do this.

And in truth, it wasn't a hardship, was it? Stroking up and down Ezog's huge, pulsing weight, feeling its velvety softness beneath her fingers, feeling a smudge of hot liquid pooling onto her palm as she brushed against its rounded tip. At where the head of him was still fully hidden, enclosed beneath its hood of greenish skin.

"Keep opening him up, my sweet," murmured Tryg beside her—and after another ragged, gulping breath, Lydia nodded, and obeyed. Watching as her audacious fingers gently drew that soft skin back, revealing what was waiting beneath.

And—oh, gods, it was just as compelling as the rest of it. A blunt, glossy green crown, split with a deep, perfect slit. A slit that was already dripping, dangling a long, pearly strand of white...

"So pretty, is he not?" Tryg's heated voice said. "You like, my sweet pet?"

Lydia swallowed, and jerked a furtive, trembly nod. And when she risked a glance up at Tryg's face, he was watching her with clear approval, his eyes glittering in the firelight. "Good," he murmured. "Very, very good. Now, you wish for more?"

Damn it, Lydia *did* wish for more, her greedy gaze already snapping back toward Ezog again. Toward where he was still standing there, unmoving, his eyes now utterly rapt on hers. As if he wanted more, too.

So she... kept going. Kept stroking, kept learning this strange, hideous orc. First caressing her fingers all over his stunning cock, and then slipping down to his full, softly furred bollocks below. And then a little way down his solid, muscled thighs—also covered with thick black hair—and then back up to the ridges of his hard abdomen, his chest. His skin feeling impossibly warm and smooth beneath the tentative touch of her fingers, despite the nicks and knots of his many scars.

And when Tryg reached an easy hand, and turned Ezog around, she felt her breath catching at the sight of it. At his broad, powerful shoulders, his scarred muscled back, the firm roundness of his arse below. This was all... *hers*. For her use, and her pleasure.

So she touched Ezog's back too, all the way up to his shoulders, brushing against the shining fall of his hair. And then, with a burst of inexplicable courage, she skated her hands very lightly over his arse, feeling the hard rounded strength of it. Her touch becoming smoother, steadier, with every breath—at least, until Tryg's hand settled over hers, and gently guided it between those firm arse-cheeks.

Ezog twitched and gasped at that, and Tryg gave a low, satisfied laugh as he eased Lydia's finger a little closer. Against where she could feel Ezog clenching back toward her... and then softening, opening. As if he would truly welcome her there, too...

"He's real sweet inside, too," Tryg murmured. "Deep and tight and hot, ach?"

Wait. Wait, did Tryg mean he'd—*oh*. And once again, Lydia was fighting to swallow down her shock, and perhaps even her jealousy, because he still wanted to—to share this with her. Together. Right?

And Tryg's eyes on her were searching again, testing again, as he carefully nudged her finger further inside. *Inside Ezog*, oh hell, to where he was indeed hot and tight and silky smooth, clamping gently around her finger. Firing a sudden, inexplicable jolt of heat to Lydia's groin, especially when Tryg drew his own hand away, and left hers there. Left her touching her gift, inside her gift, learning what he had to offer...

"You like?" Tryg breathed, his voice rasping. "He's good, ach?"

And yes, yes, he was. Because Ezog was just allowing Lydia *inside* him like this, allowing her this touch, this exploration, this familiarity. This strange, vivid reassurance that she really was the one in charge here, and that he would truly welcome whatever she wanted, and do only what she wished.

So Lydia nodded, jerky and quick, meeting Tryg's eyes. Seeing the sharp, glittering hunger in them as he gently drew her hand away, and then turned Ezog back around. Again confronting her with his hideous face, and his huge, beautiful cock, swollen perhaps even fuller than before.

"He's a good gift, ach?" Tryg continued, with more challenge on his heated voice. "You like? Wish to now put him to good use?"

And again, somehow, Lydia was nodding. *Nodding*, and meaning it, more and more with every shaky, desperate breath. Yes. *Yes*.

"Yes," she whispered. "Yes, please."

6

Even despite her agreement, Lydia had no conception whatsoever of what came next. Of how to put an orc—a whole living, thinking being— to... *good use*.

But thankfully, Tryg once again took charge of the situation. First guiding Lydia over toward the bed, and then kicking off his own trousers. Revealing the familiar sight of his tall scarred body, markedly leaner and greyer than Ezog's, the hair smattered across his skin all gone silver.

And yes, there was his own swollen cock, too, jutting out hard and pointed and slim—but Lydia only had an instant to look before Tryg dropped to sit on the fur-covered bed, and swept her bodily down into his lap.

"Mayhap we keep this pretty frock for now," he purred into her ear, as he caressed her breast through the silky red fabric. "This way, you'll think most upon how this feels, ach?"

How this feels. Because wait, Tryg was already tugging up Lydia's dress, and shifting her tighter on his lap, so his hard, jabbing strength was pressed long against her bare arse beneath her skirts. And then—her breath choked—he beckoned purposefully toward Ezog, and pointed him... toward the floor before them.

And oh, hell, Ezog instantly nodded, and obliged. Striding over toward them without a twitch of hesitation, and falling to his knees on the hard wood. While Tryg's familiar, capable hands found Lydia's thighs beneath her skirts, and slowly began easing them apart.

"Now, what do you wish for first, pet," Tryg murmured. "Mayhap my sweet *elskan* shall open you up for me? Give you a taste of his clever tongue?"

Lydia's disbelief was surging again—Tryg couldn't truly *want* that, could he? But twisting around to look at his face, she realized that his eyes were glittering, his lips parted, his black tongue sweeping against them. As if... yes. Yes, he really, really wanted that.

And maybe she did too, oh hell, and she jerked a shaky-feeling nod. To which Tryg gave one of those low, approving chuckles, as he drew her thighs further apart, opening her up wide beneath her skirts. And then—Lydia froze, caught, breathless—he reached for Ezog's ugly head, and guided it up under the hanging red fabric.

And—oh. *Oh*. Warm breath, ghosting between her legs. Gentle hands, settling high on her inner thighs. And then—then—a light, tentative brush of something slick and soft and alive.

Ezog's *tongue*.

"Oh gods," Lydia gasped, as Tryg again chuckled beneath her, and spread her thighs even wider. And then he slid his big hands upwards, over her dress, curving against her belly, finding her breasts. While that slick slippery heat under her skirts just kept stroking, tasting, caressing. Touching again and again with astonishing gentleness, easing her open upon that light, stunning touch.

"You like?" Tryg murmured, his hands kneading and squeezing, his own hot mouth kissing and nipping up the side of Lydia's shoulder. Already working with far more hardness and purpose than Ezog's steady, careful licks, and the contrast felt so strange, almost obscene. Especially when Tryg's firm hand tilted Lydia's face sideways, so he could find her mouth with his. Kissing her with eager, powerful hunger, his tongue already seeking deep inside, while Ezog's tongue below had scarcely begun to delve within.

But oh, it felt so good, impossibly good. Those two clever mouths working at once upon her, teasing her open for them, while she trembled and squirmed and gasped. And somehow even felt herself easing closer toward the bottom tongue, pressing back against it, wanting more, needing more, oh.

And yes, yes, it was instantly obliging, following just what she wished. Seeking deeper, harder, but still slow and succulent, as though savouring every taste. While Tryg's mouth was still sharp and ravenous, his teeth scraping her lips, wringing up the hunger higher, harder, closer, already—

But then Tryg yanked back, searching Lydia's face with bright, glinting eyes—and below, that softly stroking tongue had stopped, too. Perhaps waiting for Tryg's next command, just the same way Lydia was—and oh, Tryg was grasping for the hem of her dress, and smoothly drawing it upward.

"You won't mind seeing my *elskan* now, ach?" he murmured. "Now that you ken how good he feels?"

Oh. And even as Lydia belatedly cringed at her own reluctance to see Ezog—and the fact that Tryg had clearly known it, too—she felt herself actually helping him, pulling up both her dress and her shift over her head. And once she'd tossed it all away, there was only the impossible, inevitable sight of Ezog's face. Hovering close and hideous between her spread thighs, his torn, broken mouth streaked all over with shiny wetness. With... *her.*

But perhaps Tryg had been right, because no matter how Ezog's face looked, his tongue had felt so, *so* good—and the sight of Tryg's hand on his head like that, guiding him forward into Lydia's wide-open heat, was doing strange, shuddering things inside her. Things that found her actually clenching at Ezog's seeking tongue, as though kissing back at it, oh gods, needing more, deeper, yes—

"Ach, that's it, *elskan*," Tryg's low voice ordered. "Open her for me. Ready her for my strong Skai ploughing."

Ezog's moan shuddered up into Lydia's very core, his tongue's gentle, inexorable press deepening, widening. Indeed as if he fully intended to... *open* her, for Tryg. And yes, Tryg was even shifting Lydia upon him again, so that he could free his cock from beneath her, its hard jabbing length pointing straight toward Ezog's face...

And as Lydia stared, utterly caught, Ezog eased sideways, and pressed a soft, open-mouthed kiss to the tapered head of Tryg's familiar, rigid cock. His hand slipping up to circle it as he kissed, clutching that scarred base with gentle fingers—and then he carefully guided that hard, hungry tip up into Lydia's quivering, waiting, wide-open heat.

"*Oh*," she gasped, whimpered, as she felt Tryg's slick length carving into her. Sliding in so swift and easy, because Ezog had already opened and softened her for it. And as Ezog knelt there, watching Tryg sink inside, his lashes fluttered, his lips parting, a low groan rumbling from his throat. Until Tryg had sunk himself all the way in, pressing up deep—and then Ezog leaned forward again, kissing and licking and tasting. Not just against Lydia now, but against Tryg, too.

But it still felt so, so good. So impossibly, wonderfully decadent, to have Tryg's strength jutted inside her, grinding up again and again, while Ezog's brilliant warm mouth licked and caressed upon them. Not seeming to care in the slightest how it looked, how it tasted, how it sounded, or even—Lydia gasped—how Tryg's increasingly powerful thrusts had slipped him out of her entirely, his rigid wet length slapping hard against Ezog's face.

But Ezog only lifted his hooded eyes up, and sucked Tryg's glistening, dripping cockhead inside his mouth. And when Tryg's big hand curved against the back of his head, pulling him forward, Ezog swallowed him deep with damnable ease, that full scarred shaft vanishing swift and smooth between his eager, sucking lips.

It was yet another impossibly shocking sight, another twitch of jealousy, or maybe even shame. Because even Lydia's best attempts at pleasuring Tryg had gotten nowhere near this, right? And surely she must have been a pathetic disappointment, in comparison?

But perhaps Tryg had followed that, because his arm abruptly tightened around her waist, his breath hissing hot and close in her ear. "My *elskan* is so sweet, ach, pet?" he whispered. "An' so pretty, with his mouth so full of Skai prick."

And again, Tryg was... sharing this with her. Wanting her to be part of it. And Lydia had to gulp for air, find words, find truth amidst the chaos. "Yes, he's—very sweet," she whispered back. "No wonder you like him so much."

Beneath her, Tryg's body twitched, almost as if surprised—but then he nodded, and his hand slipped down to Ezog's sweaty, hideous face, still stuffed full of his jabbing cock. And Tryg exhaled a slow sigh as his hand stroked against Ezog's scarred cheek, caressing it as though it was something prized, something precious.

"Ach, I do like him," he murmured. "Always have, ach?"

Ezog was blinking back up toward Tryg with blatant reverence in his expressive eyes, and Lydia could see his tongue and throat working, as if desperately attempting to convey his own affection, his own appreciation. And Tryg liked it, he wanted it, his body heaving beneath Lydia's, his hand still caressing Ezog's face with such soft, unabashed tenderness.

"Ach, enough, *elskan*," he breathed, and Ezog instantly drew back again, his eyes downcast, as Tryg's hard, scarred length slowly extended from his mouth. Until it had bobbed fully free again, and Ezog gently guided it back inside Lydia, his eyes fluttering as he leaned forward, and again pressed his lips against their joined bodies.

But even as the pleasure surged and swayed, rising with every sharp plunge of Tryg's hips beneath her, Lydia seemed caught in it, somehow, trapped in the power of that previous moment. And she felt her trembling hands slipping downwards, their tentative touch instantly twitching Ezog backwards, his eyes wide and uncertain—but then she drew Tryg's strength out again, and pointed it toward Ezog's hideous, blinking face.

"Again, if you would," she choked out. "He's right. You were just—so pretty, with him inside you."

She didn't miss the shock in Ezog's eyes, and then his shy, furtive little nod, as he again sucked Tryg deep. While beneath Lydia, Tryg gasped and groaned, his face suddenly buried in her neck, his teeth scraping hard. And his clever fingers had slipped down to where his cock had been, easing up inside her, and there was the feel of another finger easing in, too. Ezog's finger, oh hell, as his eyes blinked up at her with worshipful gratitude, his mouth still sucking greedily around Tryg's cock.

"You don't mind—if I grant him—my seed?" Tryg was gasping, his breaths hitching into her throat. "Oughta be— yours, sweet thing."

But Lydia's hand was reaching up behind her, catching against the back of Tryg's head, drawing him down closer, as both orcs' fingers twisted and tangled together inside her. "No," she gasped back. "Want him—you—both of you—to have it. A gift."

Tryg again groaned into her neck, his teeth scraping— and then he bit down, hard, as he bucked up powerfully beneath her, and poured out deep into Ezog's tight sucking throat. Into where Ezog's previously hideous face looked almost beatific, alight with pleasure and joy, as his throat convulsed again and again and again. In strange, syncing time with Tryg's hard, hungry swallows against Lydia's ear, and then—she jerked, flailed, cried out—with her own fierce, desperate release, pulsing around the orcs' fingers. The sensation so strong and staggering that the room reeled away, and there was only white wailing ecstasy, screaming and shattering behind her eyes.

And then... stillness. Shaky, trembling stillness, holding all three of them locked together. Tryg's teeth sunk in Lydia's neck, his cock buried in Ezog's throat, and both their fingers still thrust deep inside her. While their breaths heaved, thick and heavy, almost as one.

It was finally Tryg who drew away first, gently extracting his teeth from Lydia's skin, and giving it a soft, lingering kiss. While between their legs, Ezog slowly pulled back too, easing Tryg's shiny, much-subdued length from his mouth, until it fell down slack and still. And then Ezog slid out his finger, and Tryg's too, only to replace them with... his mouth. His gentle, reverent mouth, kissing her there with exquisite, aching sweetness.

"Th-thank you," Lydia whispered, once Ezog had drawn away again, his eyes shimmering as they flicked between her and Tryg. "That was just so—lovely."

Behind her, Tryg gave a low, strange-sounding growl, his lips again kissing at where he'd bitten her neck. "Ach," he said, hoarse. "So sweet, both of you. So good. *Ach.*"

Lydia found her eyes meeting Ezog's, her mouth twitching up almost in perfect time with his. In perfect accord, somehow, because they'd done this together, earning Tryg's pleasure, or perhaps even his awe. And Lydia felt her own hand slipping to Ezog's silken head too, curling there with almost familiar-feeling ease. With... affection.

"What—should you wish for next?" came Tryg's voice, low and unsteady against Lydia's throat. "Whatever you wish, sweet thing."

Oh. Lydia shivered all over, her eyes still holding to Ezog, searching him. Seeing the warmth, and the hunger, and the... longing. Wanting more, more, just like she did. For them, yes, and for... Tryg. For the orc they both... loved.

"I think... I'd like to have more of my... gift," she whispered, toward Ezog's eyes. "As much as he'd like to give me."

Ezog's eyes widened, looking genuinely astonished, and behind her, she could hear Tryg's harsh hiss, the catch in his throat. "But... I ken my *elskan* would like to plough you, sweet pet," he said, choked. "I ken he'd like to fill your womb with his fat perfect prick, and his good sweet seed."

Oh. And yes, yes, Ezog was nodding, hard and fervent, his eyes still shocked on Lydia's face. Again, as if this was a gift for him, not her. And she felt herself softly smiling, her hand stroking tighter against his head, her thumb even brushing his scarred, hideous cheek.

"Would you?" she whispered. "Please?"

And oh, the look in his eyes. Reverent, worshipful, shifting with wonder and awe. With joy.

"Ach, woman," he breathed. "I shall."

7

Lydia didn't know who moved first, or whether it was all three of them at once. But somehow, she found herself lying sprawled on her back on the bed, with Tryg stretched out long beside her, and Ezog's huge, scarred body kneeling over her.

And for the briefest of instants, blinking up at that close, horrifyingly hideous face, there was again a twitch of fear, sparking inside Lydia's chest. Enough that Ezog abruptly stilled over her, his eyes wide and alarmed on hers—but Lydia drew in breath, and settled her shaky hands against his warm, shifting back. And then she even attempted a smile, though she couldn't help a brief, pleading look toward Tryg beside them.

And yes, Tryg was here, familiar and certain and safe, flashing them both a swift, affectionate grin. "Ach, no need to rush, my sweets," he murmured. "You must only keep learning each other, just as I've learnt both of you."

Oh. Lydia could feel Ezog's big body slightly relaxing over her, and she was relaxing too, her fingers spreading wider against his back. Earning another encouraging smile from Tryg, and she belatedly realized his hand was on Ezog's back too, stroking up and down with firm, steady reassurance.

"You shall be my *elskan*'s first woman, ach, pretty pet?" Tryg continued, his voice low. "It shall grant me great joy to give him this. To teach him how good your sweet womb shall feel, when he is buried deep inside it."

Oh, *hell*. Both Lydia and Ezog had shuddered at that, though Lydia's eyes had snapped back up to Ezog's hideous face, searching his hazy eyes. "I would be—your first?" she croaked. "Are you sure you—"

Her answer came in a guttural groan from Ezog's mouth, a hard, sustained nudge of his swollen heat against her inner thigh. Because yes, he was already there, already so close, and Lydia's breath hitched as she shifted a little beneath him, lining him up, even closer...

"Ach, that's it," murmured Tryg beside them, his eyes half-lidded as he glanced down between them. Blatantly watching, *approving*, as Ezog's hips slightly canted, prodding him just up against there, oh, *there*. "Find each other, my sweets. You can feel how open and ready she is for you, ach, *elskan*? How she kisses you, and longs to suck you in deep?"

And yes, yes, Lydia's open heat was brazenly kissing at that gently pressing hardness, longing for it, convulsing powerfully against it. As it shuddered in return, swelling even fuller, while Ezog groaned again, long and low—and then he nudged just a little deeper. Parting Lydia around that smooth rounded head, and she groaned too, arching up beneath him, spreading even wider...

"Ach, just like that," continued Tryg's soft, heated voice. "Seek it slow and easy. I ken my *elskan* shall be the largest prick you have ever known, ach, sweet thing? You shall need to make yourself wide open for him, and learn how to swallow him whole inside you."

Lydia gasped and nodded, her body frantically clamping against where Ezog's slowly sinking cock indeed felt larger, more overpowering, than anything she'd ever felt there before. But wait, that included Tryg himself, and wouldn't he be upset by that, or jealous—but another glance at his face showed his eyes still hungry and hooded, his tongue again greedily brushing his mouth.

"It grants me great joy to witness my *elskan* opening you thus," he purred at her. "I should keep no woman who could not bear him, ach? Who could not welcome his good fat prick inside her?"

Oh. Lydia's thoughts were swirling, scattering—*keep*, he'd said—and Ezog was moaning again, his eyes now squeezed shut, his slow invasion between her legs briefly gone still. Because it was already so much, oh gods, her body stretched taut and thin around him—but he was only halfway in, and she needed more, more, needed to welcome him, to open for him...

"More," she whispered at him, one of her hands somehow fluttering up to his hideous face. Snapping his eyes open again, so wide she could see the whites of them, the wild clash of pleasure and uncertainty and fear.

"Ach, more," agreed Tryg's husky voice beside them, his hand still stroking Ezog's back, sliding over Lydia's hand as it went. "My sweet *elskan* feels so good, woman, ach? So thick and fat inside you?"

Lydia fervently nodded, holding Ezog's eyes, giving him a genuine, wavering smile—and even though she could feel him swelling more inside her, he still hadn't moved again. That unease still shimmering in his eyes, as if he really wasn't sure, maybe about her, about Tryg, about this...

And without thinking, without hesitating, Lydia drew down his hideous face, and... *kissed* him. Kissed his ruined, broken mouth, with its torn lip and jagged teeth. And yes, it felt different, tasted different... but it also felt—right. Right, in the shaky relief of his exhale, in the easy, already-familiar gentleness of his tongue. The way it kissed with such soft, careful thoroughness, just like it had between her legs.

Oh, it was good, and Lydia arched up further, perhaps opened wider, welcoming him in. In both places now, her mouth and her swollen clutching heat—and yes, yes, Ezog was giving her more. Pressing in again, pushing through the stretch and the burn and the ache. Filling her whole with his huge driving cock, deeper and deeper and deeper, as his ruined mouth plundered hers, made her his own...

And as he finally sank all the way, stuffed to the hilt, that sense of rightness only grew, blooming through Lydia's chest. It was right, how he filled her utterly to the brim, locked and held tight. Right, how he slowly drew his mouth away to look at her, with such unabashed wonder in his shining eyes. And so, so right, in the heated, grateful way those eyes then glanced sideways at Tryg, his tongue brushing his lips—

And right, how Tryg reached for Ezog's head, yanked him close, and... kissed him. Kissed him with just the same fierce intensity that he'd kissed Lydia, biting hard enough that she could see a trickle of red streaking down Ezog's scarred chin.

But there wasn't even the slightest twinge of jealousy, not even at the fact that Ezog's throbbing cock was buried whole inside her, filling her to her very limit, while he so eagerly kissed someone else. While Tryg furiously kissed him back, and then—Lydia gasped—he suddenly swung his tall body up over Ezog's, so he was looking down at her over Ezog's shoulder. His eyes fiery and flashing with hunger, his teeth bared sharp and white.

"You shall not mind, sweet pet," he hissed, his breaths oddly laboured, "if I plough my *elskan* thus, ach?"

Lydia's groan was hoarse and betraying, her tongue sweeping against her lips. "Of—course not," she choked. "He feels—so *good*."

Tryg's answering nod was jerky and quick, his hand already working down between them, making Ezog gasp and arch, his eyes fluttering—and then, oh, oh, Lydia could almost *feel* Tryg finding that hot sweet tightness with his hard hungry cock, piercing it open around him. And in return, she felt Ezog's cock swelling fuller against their own already-snug fit, locking them even tighter in place, as Tryg pressed further and further inside.

"So good," Tryg gasped, his silver head thrown back, showing his long, corded, convulsing neck. "Ach, just like that. Suck me all the way in, *elskan*, so nice and tight, show me how good you are, *ach*—"

Above Lydia, Ezog was moaning too, his eyes dazed and desperate—and he jerked against her, inside her, at the telltale slap of skin against skin, at the sound of Tryg surely slamming deep. Filling Ezog, just as Ezog was filling her, and oh, it was impossible, it was unthinkable, it was utterly unreal...

"Ach, that's it," Tryg breathed, his glinting eyes darting between Ezog and Lydia, his chest heaving. "That's so good. So sweet. Both of you. Even better than I thought. *Ach*."

He'd abruptly grasped for a handful of Ezog's long hair, yanking his head back—but the flash across Ezog's eyes was only pleasure, craving, anticipation. And Tryg's mouth curled into a sly, menacing grin as he held Ezog there, as he slowly, deliberately drew out again, as Ezog's huge body quaked with the loss of it...

And then Ezog bucked and shouted as Tryg drove back inside. The impact driving him tighter into Lydia, too, and oh, it felt good, so, so *good*—and behind Ezog, Tryg was fully laughing now, his head again thrown back, his clawed grip tightening in Ezog's hair.

"Even better, my sweets," he purred at him, at her, at them, with greedy satisfaction in his glittering eyes. "Ach, you're both so pretty, aren't you? So good, when you're being ploughed together by a good Skai prick?"

Both Ezog and Lydia frantically nodded, and Lydia was even clutching Ezog closer, clinging to his warm solid safety, while Tryg drew out again, and then slammed back inside. Making them both shudder and moan, their voices rising with every powerful plunge of Tryg's hips—and Tryg's eyes were blazing now, almost feral, as he punched in again and again and again.

"So sweet," he gasped, his voice cracking. "So perfect. And you'll both be even sweeter when you're stuffed chock-full of good seed, ach? When you're both stretched wide open and leaking for me, because you're both mine, mine, *mine*—"

He'd snapped out the words with harsh, forceful thrusts, with pure flashing menace in his eyes—and with one last, vicious plunge, he was groaning, guttural and deep, as ecstasy shot across his face. As Ezog beneath him startled and shook, his eyes wide, his strength still inside Lydia quivering sharp—and then he was shouting into her neck as he sprayed out deep, too. Surging her full of his hot thick seed, flooding her every last space with him—until her own pleasure finally caught again, too. Kicking and throbbing around him, clutching him, kissing him, *thanking* him.

And perhaps Ezog was thanking her, too, moaning as he lowered his hideous face to kiss her again. And she was already arching up to meet him, to taste him, to make his gentle, generous beauty her own.

When they drew apart again, Ezog's eyes were blinking, looking very bright, as his breath shuddered again, again. And wait, perhaps that was because of Tryg, who currently had his face buried in Ezog's neck, his throat audibly gulping as he rapidly, greedily swallowed.

Oh. It was just so damned typical of him, enough that a helpless little smile twitched on Lydia's mouth—and above her, Ezog was smiling, too. Looking just as softly affectionate as she felt, and she swallowed as she searched his face, his lovely, expressive eyes.

"You're still—sure, about this?" she whispered at him. "You didn't want to—to keep him all to yourself?"

Because she somehow understood what this truly was, now, in a way she hadn't before. Tryg hadn't had other lovers. He'd had Ezog. And he loved Ezog, and perhaps he had for a long, long time.

And Ezog was still smiling down at her, so warm and tender and kind. "Ach, I am sure," he murmured back. "You have granted me great joy in this, woman. A great gift. One I have longed for all my life."

But that was perhaps a flicker of sadness in his eyes, too. And Lydia's hands were stroking at his face, seeking it, needing to know the truth of it. "But you weren't—jealous?" she whispered. "When Tryg started coming to me?"

That was definitely another shift in Ezog's eyes, a telltale swallow in his throat. "Ach, only a little," he said softly. "I knew how deeply he longed for this, and you are far from the first, ach? And he should have freely granted me leave to do the same."

Oh. Wait. So Ezog... *had* been jealous of her, then. And Tryg had—he must have asked Ezog's permission to keep seeing her, and of course Ezog had given it, because he would give anything Tryg asked. Up to and including... being a Yule gift for his new mistress. Which Ezog had readily done, down to the damned red ribbon.

"I'm—so sorry, Ezog," Lydia whispered up at him, her eyes blinking hard, as her hands stroked his face. "I would never have agreed to it, if I'd known. You deserved better."

But at that, Tryg gave an odd choking sound, and his silver head snapped up from Ezog's neck, his eyes mightily glowering down at Lydia's face. A sight that was made even more alarming by the fresh red smeared across his lips and beard, and dripping down his chin onto her shoulder.

"Ach, what's this?" he demanded, as his hand still in Ezog's hair yanked his head up, so he could frown at his face, too. "Not only did I hunt a good, sweet, lovely woman for us, but I took my good time upon this, and made sure she was all that she seemed! I tested her work and her kindness and her fealty, and her word upon whether she could share her joy with you!"

Wait. Wait, what? But Tryg was still glowering viciously between them, and giving Ezog's head a fierce little shake. "And," he continued, even harder, "I tested how she would treat you, *elskan*, with nary a warning from me! For I should never bring any woman into our life—or our bed—who might harm you, or cause you pain, or even speak a single harsh word to your perfect face!"

Oh. Oh. Was Tryg saying—this had really all been some kind of *test*? Some kind of grand scheme on his part? And— Lydia's eyes darted toward Ezog's stunned-looking face— surely he hadn't known about it, either?

"I told you again and again, *elskan*," Tryg continued

flatly, his eyes still glaring at Ezog, "I should never leave you for another. You are *mine*. You have *always* been mine."

His voice had gone dark and scathing, his long tongue licking at his reddened mouth. While Ezog's eyes fluttered closed, perhaps with pain, or relief, or both—and then they opened again. Catching on Lydia's face, holding there, almost as if drawing up courage.

"Then why," he whispered, without inflection, without looking at Tryg, "have you never offered to speak vows to me? Even after your clan altered their ways to allow this?"

Lydia was feeling fully lost, now—Tryg's clan hadn't allowed him to swear vows to Ezog?—but the words had clearly meant something to Tryg, something important. Because his body behind Ezog had jerked to utter, rigid stillness, his eyes wide and suddenly, surprisingly vulnerable on Ezog's face.

"You... wished for *vows*, from me?" he whispered. "In truth, *elskan*? I thought... I thought you yet wished for a woman."

Oh. And that was more mingled pain and regret in Ezog's eyes, a choked little laugh from his mouth. "Ach, once, mayhap," he whispered back. "But I knew this would never be mine, not with my face. And then... *you* were not mine, either."

Lydia could almost taste the sadness in his voice, could feel it deep and sickening in her belly. And surely Tryg could too, his throat convulsing, his mouth giving a tremulous little quiver.

"Ach, I was yours, *elskan*," he said thickly. "I am. And should you yet allow this, I'd be most honoured to swear vows to you. To"—he cleared his throat—"to do all within my power to grant you aught that you should wish."

At that, his eyes had darted, brief but betraying,

toward... Lydia. And too late, she found herself following the implications in those words. Because not only had this been some kind of devious scheme on Tryg's part, but he'd really sought her out—for *Ezog*? He'd done all that, seduced her, pleased her, brought her his damned *laundry*—because he'd thought that was what *Ezog* had wanted?

When perhaps—perhaps Ezog hadn't actually wanted it at all? When Ezog had just wanted—*him*?

Oh. Oh gods. Bile was rising in Lydia's throat, her stomach horribly plummeting, her eyes blinking back the sudden wetness behind them. Oh. They wanted—oh.

Each other. Not... her.

And gods, why had she even thought otherwise? Why had she ever imagined this would be hers? She should have known better, it had always been too good to be true, always...

"Right, then," she whispered, though the words broke in her throat. "I—understand. I'll go."

8

The orcs' reaction to Lydia's words was instantaneous. Not with them regretfully shoving up and ushering her out the door, as she might have expected—but instead, with Ezog bodily pinning her to the bed, his eyes snapped wide and alarmed, while Tryg's sharp, angry bark echoed through the room.

"What rubbish is this, woman?" he demanded at her, his voice harsh and malicious. "*No*, you shall not go! I have hunted you, we have ploughed you and claimed you, and thus, you are *ours*!"

Lydia blinked up toward his furious face, and then toward Ezog, who was fervently nodding, his eyes fearful and pleading. "You cannot wish to go, sweet woman," he whispered. "Not after this. Your joy tasted so sweet, ach? Have I not well pleased you, as your gift?"

Lydia couldn't stop blinking at him, at them, and she twitched a short, shaky nod. "Y-yes," she whispered back. "Of course you pleased me, Ezog. But now that I know what you really wanted... what *he* really wanted..."

She shot a furtive glance up at Tryg, who was still

looking furious—but that was more pain, more regret, flashing across Ezog's face. "Ach," he rasped. "Should you wish to go, then—you ought. We should never wish to—"

He was interrupted by Tryg's fierce, guttural growl, and a hard, high-pitched laugh from his suddenly cruel-looking mouth. "No," he hissed. "No. I won't allow it. You're here with us now, woman. You're yet stuck upon my *elskan*'s fat, perfect prick. And you won't again escape it, until I grant you my leave!"

Oh. The words rippled up Lydia's spine, strange and terrifying and wonderful—especially when Tryg grasped another handful of Ezog's hair, and yanked his head back. "Fuck her, *elskan*," he hissed. "Plough her until she screams. Teach her who she belongs to. Ach?"

Ezog's growl was vicious and deep, his body taut and poised over Lydia, as if ready to strike, to obey—but his wide eyes were frantically searching her face. Their expression again something between pain, and longing, and fear.

Because... he'd sworn to serve her. To be a gift to her. *I shall do naught you do not wish for, woman.*

And even if Tryg didn't care about the promises he'd made to her, Ezog still did. He did. And suddenly Lydia wanted to weep and beg and plead for it, she needed it, needed him to show her, please...

And she was nodding at him, quick and urgent, yes, yes, *yes, please*—even as Tryg again yanked his head back, his snarl more like a roar. "I said, plough her!" he barked in Ezog's ear. "Make her beg and *scream* for us, *elskan*. Now!"

And this time, now that Ezog had Lydia's permission, the furious hunger caught and flashed in his eyes, turning them hot and liquid and dangerous. His growl rumbling low and decadent into Lydia's belly, clamping her even tighter upon his thick invading cock as he slowly drew backwards. Emptying her breath by breath, unstoppering her, taking himself away from her, *wait*—until a hot gush of fluid spurted out, flooding against them both. Releasing the pressure, Lydia distantly realized, making room, so he could...

His slam inside was brutal, merciless, so hard she shook all over—but yes, yes, he was in her again, he was making her his, making her theirs. And his choked, triumphant growl in her ear as he ground deep inside was everything, everything, cradling her, sustaining her, even as he pulled out again, taking it away...

But then he slammed in again, even harder this time. Chattering Lydia's teeth with the impact, flashing out unmistakable pain around his huge, overpowering invasion—but she didn't care, she didn't, and she clung to him as he pummelled in again, again, again. Brutalizing her, breaking her, as the seed sloshed and spurted between them, and his cold, ruthless, terrifying eyes flashed on her face. Drinking her up, wanting to see her like this, weak and shivering and utterly overwhelmed for him, her only possible recourse to take more, to open wider, to welcome his monstrous, merciless conquest.

And Lydia needed it, craved it, revelled in it, so lost and so desperate that she almost didn't notice Tryg behind him, again plunged deep inside him, driving him even harder. "Ach, that's it," he was hissing, as he bit at Ezog's tattered ear. "Plough her as hard as you can, *elskan*. Pump that sweet little womb wide open for us. Make sure she feels that strong fat prick, make sure she knows what it shall do to her, when she *dares* to spurn my great gift!"

And oh, oh gods, Lydia's blinking streaming eyes were on Tryg's now, her head somehow shaking, despite the furious orc still pummelling her pinned, quivering body.

"Not—*spurning*," she pleaded at him. "L-loved it. J-just didn't want to—hurt him."

Tryg's eyes were flashing again, his lips pursing, as his own cock kept plunging into Ezog's arse, the sounds of sloshing liquid and slapping skin even sharper than before. "Then say this, human," he growled. "Swear this. You are his. Mine. *Ours*."

His voice seemed to strike at Lydia's heart, even deeper than his rage, deeper than the huge cock still swiving between her legs. But deeper still were Ezog's eyes, blazing on hers with such desperate longing and fury and craving. Wanting this. Taking her as brutally as he could, in the hopes that he could save this, have this. Have her.

"Yours," Lydia gasped at him, her hands finding his face, trembling uncontrollably against it as he kept plunging hard and deep. "Yours, Ezog. I swear. Yours."

And oh, his groan was both pain and pleasure, victory and helplessness, a laugh and a sob—and his face thrust into her neck as his strength inside her finally held, stayed, locked tight again, just where he belonged. And then his teeth bit down, breaking her skin, as his cock plunged even deeper—and blasted her full. Emptying itself in furious swells of sharp shuddering heat, until her own sore, stretched-out body shuddered out its relief, too. Seizing in pulse after dragging, agonizing pulse, drinking him dry and empty, until there was nothing, nothing left.

And then, finally, stillness. Strange, ringing stillness, broken only by their heaving breaths, and the crackling of the fire. And then—Lydia twitched—by a loud, obscene squelching sound, trembling through Ezog's body, as Tryg pulled himself back, and up to his knees behind Ezog again.

And gods, he looked... terrifying. With red streaked all through his face and beard, still dripping off his chin, down onto his scarred, sweaty chest. And his eyes were still glittering, dangerous, ravenous, as they lingered in the vicinity of Ezog's arse, his groin. Upon what must have been a wide-open, seed-covered, lewd-looking mess.

But Tryg liked it, he was *pleased* with it, and oh, Lydia could feel him even spreading Ezog's legs wider, blatantly giving himself a better view. "Very pretty, my sweets," he hissed, harsh and low. "Both of you rent so wide open for me. Look how sweet you are, dripping out all this good fresh seed for me."

Oh, *hell*. And he'd even bent down over Ezog's arse again, and though Lydia couldn't see what he was doing, she could feel Ezog's choked, desperate gasps into her skin as Tryg licked and slurped and worked him over, the sounds slick and crude and shameless.

But when Tryg finally arose again, he was looking supremely satisfied, his tongue licking his reddened lips as his hands caressed up and down Ezog's still-trembling flanks. "Better, *elskan*?" he murmured. "Any pain, now?"

Ezog gave a thoroughly unintelligible grunt into Lydia's throat—into where he was *still* swallowing, oh gods—and Tryg let out an amused-sounding laugh as he dropped back down beside Lydia on the bed, his clawed hand easily curving against her cheek, tilting her face toward him.

"Just grant him a spell," he murmured at her, his eyes angling fondly toward Ezog's head, still buried deep into the other side of her neck. "He's never drunk fresh from a woman before, ach? This is a great gift, you ken."

Oh. Lydia couldn't quite hide her wince at that telltale word *gift*, and she could see Tryg's smile abruptly fading, his eyes sobering. "I hope..." he began, and then grimaced, shook his head. "I'm sorry, sweet thing, if I frightened you, in this. If I... pushed you, beyond what you wished. Beyond what we... promised you."

Lydia swallowed, and somehow managed a careful shrug of her shoulder nearest him. "It isn't... that," she croaked. "It's just..."

She couldn't finish, couldn't even begin to articulate it, but Tryg nodded, and gave her a crooked, sad little smile. "Didn't tell you what I was really up to, did I?" he said, quiet. "Didn't tell you I had... other aims, in coming to you, beyond just our pleasure together."

Yes, yes, that was exactly it, and Tryg must have seen it in her eyes, because he sighed again, and wiped at his still-red mouth. "Ach. I'm sorry, sweet thing. Last thing I wished was to bring you pain. It's only"—his eyes flicked toward Ezog's head again—"I've played this fool game too oft before, ach? And even when I've been sure I won it, sure I found a good woman for us both—it's always ended with my *elskan* being hurt. And I couldn't bear it again, ach? Swore to Skai-kesh that I'd try one last time, but I wasn't letting any of it *near* my sweet *elskan* until I was sure."

Oh. Skai-kesh was the patron god of Tryg's Skai clan, Lydia knew, and he huffed another sigh, caressed his hand against her hot cheek. "An' I begged, again and again, for a good one," he whispered. "A woman just as soft and sweet and gentle as my own *elskan*. And"—his chest filled, hollowed—"Skai-kesh heard me, sweet thing, and blessed me. Gave me a great, great gift, in you."

Lydia still couldn't seem to find words for this, though her eyes were blinking hard, a strange stilted hopefulness skittering in her chest. And Tryg drew in breath, stroking her cheek again, as his mouth pulled into a wavering, uncertain little smile.

"Really do want to keep you, sweet thing," he continued,

even quieter. "For myself, and for my *elskan*, too. You've brought him such joy this night, and I ken you'll bring him far more, ach? It's a rare human who sees past his face, to all the sweetness inside. An' to see you treat him so tenderly, and then turn about and squeal so sweetly upon his perfect prick's ploughing"—he shrugged, his grin hitching higher—"this was one of the greatest sights in all my life, ach?"

The shimmering hopefulness kept fluttering stronger in Lydia's chest, and Tryg's smile twitched even higher, his eyes so warm, so affectionate. "Mayhap you'll think more upon this, sweet thing," he murmured, "whilst I give you better cause to forgive me, ach?"

And before Lydia could attempt a reply, Tryg's lean body shoved downwards again, and he purposefully nudged sideways at Ezog's arse. And though Ezog didn't draw his mouth from Lydia's neck, he shifted a little over her, and then slowly, carefully drew his softened cock out of her sore, tender heat. And once again, it was followed by a thick, spurting rush of molten seed, gushing out from inside her, and into...

Tryg's *mouth*?!

Lydia's moan was deep and desperate, her eyes wide and shocked on the sight. On Tryg's face pressed tight between her legs, his throat audibly gulping, while his greedy eyes glittered bright and challenging on her face.

"Oh," Lydia gasped, because there were truly no other words, not with two ravenous orcs feasting upon her at once. With Ezog still drinking from her neck, while Tryg loudly, eagerly sucked and swallowed between her legs. Drinking Ezog's thick, copious fresh seed out from inside her, his tongue licking and caressing, sending out furious flares of sharp, sparkling bliss.

And when Lydia's moans rose almost to screams, almost

to the edge, Tryg only barked a satisfied laugh, and kissed her, and promptly drew away. Leaving her gasping and untouched and trembling all over—until he nudged Ezog back on top again. Guiding that fat, hungry cock back inside her, wanting it to fill her again, perhaps so he could drink out more...

And Ezog instantly obliged, moaning into Lydia's neck as he rocked softly into her, moving easy and slow this time, while she arched and shouted beneath him, her release wracking through them both. Once again dragging out more furious bursts of seed from Ezog, pouring her tight and full—and then Tryg elbowed Ezog aside, and knelt low between her legs. Again making stunning, spectacular use of his tongue, until she was left dizzy and boneless and incoherent, gulping desperately for breath.

At that point, Tryg kissed them both, and then shoved himself up, and went to collect a waterskin. First pouring it out into Lydia's mouth, and then—after a gentle but firm command—drawing Ezog away from Lydia's neck, so he could pour it out down his throat, too. And once Ezog had emptied the waterskin, he gave Tryg a long, grateful-looking kiss, and then eased back up over Lydia, sliding himself deep between her legs. Holding her eyes as he gently rocked inside her, his tongue reverently licking at his reddened lips.

"You shall now forgive our Skai, ach, sweet woman?" he murmured, as his deep, soulful eyes shimmered and shone on hers. "I ken he ought not to have hidden this truth from you, but now that you have gained his trust and his favour, he shall not falter in his care for you, ach?"

His slow thrusts inside her seemed to settle the words deeper, stronger—and Lydia clung to him, to the quiet reassurance of his big, powerful body, all over her, around her, within her.

"But he still—hid it—from you, too," she somehow pointed out, between her gasping breaths. "Still didn't tell you—why he came—to *me*."

But Ezog's expression didn't change in the slightest, and perhaps it even softened as he glanced sideways, toward where Tryg was intently watching them, his eyes glittering. "Ach, but you see, this was part of his care for me," Ezog murmured. "And when you love a Skai, as we do, you must understand that their care for you stands above all else, ach? Even above their truth."

That still seemed highly questionable, to Lydia's mind, but Ezog was still smiling like that toward Tryg, with such raw, powerful affection in his eyes. "It is best only to trust them," he continued, "and to know that they shall never leave you behind."

Oh. Best... to *trust* them. And as much as the unease kept twisting in Lydia's belly, she couldn't deny the startling familiarity in those words, either. The way she'd always implicitly trusted Tryg, too. And oh, the way Tryg was looking back at Ezog, his eyes rapt and reverent, as though he was the most beautiful sight he'd ever seen in all his life.

"Never leave you behind, *elskan*," he breathed. "*Never*."

Well. And Ezog clearly believed that, because his eyes had fluttered, his cock thrusting up deeper—and then he sprayed out into Lydia again, moaning husky and low, while Tryg flashed him a smug, approving grin.

"Or you, pretty pet," he murmured toward Lydia, as he again nudged Ezog aside, and knelt between her thighs. "You shall see, ach?"

Lydia couldn't seem to argue, especially once Tryg had again begun shamelessly feasting between her legs, flashing out yet more dizzying, dazzling pleasure. And once he'd finished, he shoved Ezog onto his back, and proceeded to suck him with deft, familiar ease, too. Fitting nearly all of that massive green heft into his mouth, his eyes glimmering with wicked satisfaction as Ezog helplessly gasped and groaned beneath his touch.

Lydia was watching it too, from where Ezog had pulled her close, her head tucked against his solid shoulder. And though she'd never once imagined herself watching something like this—watching her lover sucking another orc down his throat—she found that she couldn't seem to pull her eyes away. Couldn't seem to keep from snuggling closer into Ezog's embrace, breathing in the sweet scent of his neck.

"He's so clever, isn't he?" she murmured toward him, as she watched his big clawed hand stroking against Tryg's hair. "So quick and kind and capable."

"Ach," Ezog murmured back, between gasps, as he turned his head to press a soft kiss to her forehead. "I have longed for him since the first day I saw him fight, ach? And he could have chosen any lover he wished—he did, for a long time—but—"

His voice broke there, his hips canting up, and he groaned, long and sustained, as his cock visibly pulsed between Tryg's tight lips—and yes, Tryg was greedily swallowing, his eyes fluttering on Ezog's as he sucked him dry, as he drew out every last drop.

"But then *you* caught my eye, sweet thing," Tryg said, his voice hoarse, once he'd pulled off again, licking at his slick lips. "An' then I couldn't keep myself away, ach?"

It sounded familiar, it *was* familiar, and Ezog pressed another soft, reassuring kiss to Lydia's forehead. "And he has not stopped in his care for me, ever since," he told her. "So now, you shall trust him to care for you also."

He spoke as though it was settled, decided, and

perhaps—perhaps it was. Because when Tryg gave a meaningful glance toward Lydia, and then toward Ezog's cock—which was somehow already swollen full again—she gave a quick, grateful nod, and then slid herself on top of him, her legs straddling wide. To where Tryg was lifting that fat length, nudging it up into her wet heat, and then guiding her down upon it. While beneath her, Ezog spasmed and moaned, his eyes flicking awed and worshipful between them.

And when Tryg eased close behind Lydia, his prodding rigid tip jutting further up her open crease, she didn't flinch or resist. Instead, she exhaled and tilted herself back, opened as wide as she could for him, welcoming him inside—and then shuddered and shouted at the impossible screeching sensation of it, of two orcs seeking inside her at once, making her their own.

"Ach, that's it," Tryg was purring approvingly behind her, as he fed himself in a little deeper. "You suck me deep inside you, sweet thing. You squeeze me strong and tight, whilst you also seize my *elskan's* perfect prick with your perfect little womb, ach?"

Both Lydia and Ezog were frantically nodding, holding one another's eyes, and Tryg barked a satisfied-sounding laugh behind them, and pushed in further. "So pretty," he continued, his voice catching, as his strong hands flexed against Lydia's hips, and that invading strength sank deeper, deeper, deeper. "So sweet. And you're gonna smell even sweeter when you're both stuffed full of my fresh Skai seed, ach? When you're both walking around here reeking of *me*."

His voice sharpened at the end, because oh, he was all the way in, now, jamming Lydia full, fuller than she'd ever been in her life. With two entire orcs buried inside her, filling her, claiming her, forever—

"An' *you*, sweet thing," Tryg continued, his voice a deep, certain rasp, as he gave one of Lydia's breasts a brief, proprietary squeeze. "Look how good you are. Look how pretty you are, with two orcs swallowed whole inside you. Now, you shall suck out our good seed for us, ach? You shall drink it deep within, and keep it there, so you shall always reek of our scents together, ach? So you shall always be *ours*."

And yes, yes, that was exactly what Lydia wanted, what she needed, always—and she was nodding, Ezog was nodding, she was even leaning down to kiss him again, to feel the certain strength in his lips and tongue. The way his own hips were bucking up faster, filling her fuller, while Tryg did the same behind, and it was whirling, it was singing, it was breath and light and home—and she arched up as they poured her full, as they gifted her with their good seed, their safety, their care. As she shook and shivered and wept, drank it all up with her own clutching, greedy grasp, until the deed was finally finished, sworn into stunning, staggering truth.

And when she collapsed down onto Ezog, he easily caught her, folding her into his strong arms, into his heart. "Ours, sweet woman," he whispered, so soft. "Ours, now. From this Yule onward."

And all Lydia could do was nod, and breathe, and settle in deep. "Yes," she whispered. "From this Yule onward."

9

When Lydia awoke the next morning, she was sore, and sticky, and sprawled wide on a soft, equally sticky fur. While a succulent, delicious scent wafted through the air, something like... frying meat?

And wait. Wait. Lydia's eyes snapped open, and once again found the cozy little cabin. Now with bright morning sun streaming through its small windows, illuminating where Tryg was standing by the fireplace, wearing only a pair of low-slung trousers, and flipping something in a pan. While Ezog bustled around the little table, which seemed to be piled far higher than before. With what looked like treats, and bottles of cider and ale, and... wrapped packages?

Ezog's big body had abruptly stilled, his eyes glancing toward Lydia in the bed—and for a choked, frozen moment, Lydia stared at him, and at his face. At where it was even more hideous in the bright light, all those scars and rips and imperfections on shocking, unnerving display. And for another strange, startled instant, it seemed utterly unthinkable that she had caressed him, kissed him, found such impossible pleasure with him...

But wait, that was already unease, and maybe even hurt, simmering in his watching eyes. And before she'd quite realized it, Lydia shoved her sticky body out of bed, and walked unsteadily toward him. Reaching for that broken, beautiful face, and pulling it down, and giving it a fierce, purposeful kiss.

"Morning," she said shyly, once she'd drawn away. "Happy Yule, Ezog."

Her cheeks felt very hot, suddenly, and then even hotter at the look of abject, unabashed awe in Ezog's blinking eyes. "A-ach," he stammered, his voice thick. "To—to you also, woman."

Lydia's face flushed even hotter, and thankfully she was soon rescued by Tryg, who came over with a smug, indulgent grin on his face. "You are both so shy and sweet, my pretty pets," he said, with satisfaction, as he tilted Lydia's face up for a brief, biting kiss, too. "Now, *elskan*, mayhap you shall ask our woman if you can empty that good load you've been nursing into her? And then help her bathe and dress for the day?"

His hand had dropped to grip teasingly at the obvious bulge in Ezog's trousers, even as he gave Lydia a sly, knowing wink. "He's been eyeing your pretty form all this morn, sweet thing," he informed her. "Could scarce hear a word I spoke, ach?"

With that, Tryg casually strode back to the fireplace, swiping for his pan. And Lydia could have sworn that Ezog's deep green cheeks were flushing too, his hand rubbing shyly at the back of his neck. "Sh-should you?" he said, with a wince. "Wish for—more? From—me?"

But Lydia was already nodding, her body shivering with

nervousness, or anticipation. And when Ezog led her back to the bed, she willingly climbed onto her hands and knees, and gasped as she felt gentle hands carefully opening her up, spreading her apart. And then that plump, already-familiar cock slowly, gently eased itself inside, while she moaned and shuddered around it.

Despite all the pleasures they'd enjoyed the night before, they hadn't done it from behind like this, and it distantly occurred to Lydia that perhaps Ezog didn't want her to look at his face in the bright daylight. But it still felt so, so good, so strong and safe and all-consuming, and she couldn't help glancing over her shoulder toward him as she gasped and groaned.

"Please, Ezog," she begged. "*Please.*"

And yes, yes, he was nodding, his strength plunging in once, twice, again—and his big hands spasmed on her hips as his eyes rolled back, and he sprayed out deep inside. While from across the room, there was a bright, amused-sounding cackle—and here was Tryg again, grinning fondly back and forth between them.

"Finished already, *elskan*?" he said cheerfully, as he nudged Ezog with his elbow, and untied his own trousers. "Still time for me to have a turn, then, ach?"

And wait, yes, Ezog's full strength was slipping out of her, releasing the now-familiar gush of liquid—but it was only a breath before Tryg's hot, rigid cock stabbed inside instead. Feeling so much harder and more demanding, sloshing the slick seed out messy around it, but he clearly didn't care, judging by the low, satisfied growl in his throat.

"Ach, that's good," he breathed, as he began plunging in, sinking into his usual swift, powerful rhythm. "Ach. Ploughing my woman's sweet womb, bathing my strong Skai prick in my *elskan*'s good fresh seed. Ach, you have opened her up so nice, *elskan*, made her so soft and slick for me. So sweet. *Ach*."

His voice broke, and suddenly he was spraying out, too. His cock pulsing and grinding inside as he flooded Lydia full of more hot fluid, his head tilted back, his claws digging into her hips.

But then, too quickly, he was gone—and where he'd been, there was more surging, spurting mess. Pouring out in a humiliating rush from between Lydia's parted, trembling thighs, while both orcs just stood there, and watched.

Lydia's cheeks were burning, her chagrined eyes blinking back to where—oh. Ezog's face looked even redder than before, his throat visibly convulsing, while Tryg licked his lips, and gave Lydia's arse-cheek a brief, approving little squeeze.

"So pretty, aren't you, my sweet?" he murmured approvingly. "After your sweet womb has drawn out two good fat loads, and now overflows with our fresh seed?"

Ezog rapidly nodded as he held Lydia's eyes, and he was already drifting back toward her, as if he might welcome a second round—until Tryg elbowed him in the side, and shot him another jaunty grin. "Later, *elskan*," he said lightly. "Want her ready to meet m'boy, ach?"

Ezog nodded again at that, giving Lydia a shy, sheepish smile. And once Tryg had gone back to the fire, Ezog carefully helped Lydia up, and then led her over around the bed, to where there was a large, steaming washbasin.

"I have heated you a bath," he said softly. "I should be honoured to help you bathe, unless you..."

He glanced away, the unease again far too clear in his eyes, and Lydia smiled up toward him, and leaned in close. "I'd be very happy to have your help," she replied. "Thank you, Ezog."

His answering smile was shy, and almost painfully grateful. But as he helped Lydia into the bath, and gently began stroking her with a soft soapy cloth, she could almost feel his ease returning, the steady warmth rising in his eyes.

"Do you feel any pain, from last eve?" he murmured, as he stroked against her collarbones and shoulders, and then down her arms. "Or any... regrets?"

Lydia didn't have any regrets, although she was vaguely surprised to discover she didn't feel any actual pain, either. "Just a little sore all over, maybe," she said, with a wry smile. "I'm not used to such... vigorous activity, I suppose."

Ezog smiled back, slow and fond, as his hand very carefully slipped down to one of her breasts. "It was... very good of you," he said, quiet. "To give us such gifts, when this was meant only to be a gift to you."

Lydia swallowed, and met his kind, expressive eyes. "It was a gift to me, too," she replied. "*You* were a gift, Ezog. You, and Tryg. I... I've been... so lonely, for such a long time."

Ezog's eyes were sad now, sympathetic, and too late, Lydia heard the implication in her words. Or perhaps even the... obligation.

"But you mustn't—feel as though that means anything," she choked at him. "It's only been—one night. And you and Tryg have clearly been together for—well. And he wasn't honest with either of us, and if you decide I'm not what you'd—prefer, of course I—"

Gods, what was she even saying, and she couldn't seem to finish, shaking her head back and forth. "And you should know, I'm—awful at talking," she continued. "Always saying the wrong thing, or not finding anything to say at all, so—"

She stopped there, breathing hard, bracing herself for Ezog's mockery, his judgement, something—but to her genuine surprise, he was smiling again, as his hand slid to caress her other breast, too. "Then do not speak, should you not wish," he replied. "Your truth is yet clear in your eyes and your touch and your scent, ach?"

Oh. Lydia gulped in a shaky breath, but, predictably, couldn't seem to reply—and Ezog just kept smiling, caressing down her sides, over her belly. "And ach, I wish for you," he continued, quieter. "Tryg knows all that I am, ach? He knows what I most longed for in a woman, and now, he has freely granted it to me. And"—his eyes searched hers, the unease again rising in them—"you have welcomed our claim and our seed, ach? So this is done, you ken. Settled. You are *ours*. From this Yule onward."

Lydia's words still wouldn't come, but she was urgently nodding, and Ezog nodded too, as more warmth flickered across his eyes. "And I have brought you more gifts, should you wish," he murmured. "Tryg is not oft one to think of these things, but I hope they shall please you, ach?"

Lydia couldn't hide her spark of interest at that, and Ezog grinned back at her, the sight both alarming and endearing on his face. And once he'd finished washing and drying her, he carefully dressed her in the red dress—which he'd aired out, too—before guiding her over to the loaded-up table.

"I have brought you three kinds of cider to try, and two wines," he said shyly, as he waved at the table's contents. "And some plums, and sweet breads, and puddings. And I was not sure if you should wish for a Skai gift, or jewels, so I have brought both, ach?"

With that, he thrust out one of the cloth-wrapped packages toward her—but at that moment, Tryg strode back over with a large, steaming platter of fried meat, eggs, greens, and mushrooms. "Ach, you brought her a Skai gift, *elskan*?" he asked, with undeniable curiosity, as he plunked the platter down in the middle of the table. "But I told you, our woman is too sweet to be Skai, ach? She shall be Bautul, like you."

Lydia wasn't following again, especially when Ezog's face flushed, his smile toward Tryg shy but grateful. "Ach, I ken," he said. "But I thought you should welcome this."

This, it turned out, once Lydia had unwrapped the cloth, was a slim, shining steel dagger, encased in a beautifully stamped leather scabbard. And Tryg's eyes indeed lit up at the sight of it, and he enthusiastically snatched it from Lydia's hand, inspecting the blade with a critical eye. "Ach, it matches yours, *elskan*!" he said delightedly. "Did you have Argarr forge this for her? So thoughtful, my sweet!"

Tryg looked truly thrilled by this development, and Lydia couldn't help laughing as she took the dagger back, and gingerly drew it out of its leather scabbard. "I have... never touched a weapon before," she confessed toward Ezog, with a wince. "In my life."

But the warmth kept shimmering in Ezog's eyes, and he passed another similar-looking package across the table toward Tryg. "Just as well," he said lightly. "I ken Tryg shall take great joy in teaching you, ach?"

With that, Ezog began loading up Lydia's plate with Tryg's delicious-smelling cooking, while Tryg swiftly unwrapped his own package, and again crowed with delight. And Lydia wasn't at all surprised to see that it was another dagger, though this one was far sharper and more deadly-looking, with only a slight jut of steel for a hilt, and a pointed, gleaming tip.

"Ach, is this Argarr's new throwing design, *elskan*?!" Tryg demanded, his eyes sparkling—and without warning, he flipped the dagger in his hand, and hurled it across the room. To where—Lydia's mouth dropped open—it stuck point-first into the wooden doorframe, its hilt end shuddering with the impact.

"Ach, look at that!" Tryg exclaimed, as he leapt up and rushed over to pluck it out of the wood—only to hurl it back across the room, to where it sank deep into the opposite wall. "Perfect weight and balance, *elskan*! I did not yet own one, thus!"

Ezog was beaming toward Tryg, his eyes bright and indulgent. "I thought this should please you," he told him, as he went to collect two more plates from the shelf, and then began loading them up with food, too. "Now, go greet our guests, ach?"

Tryg had already whirled around toward the door, flinging it wide open, because—oh. There were two more orcs, standing in the snow just outside. They were both younger-looking orcs, and one of them was laughing with rather Tryg-like glee, and hurling himself bodily into Tryg's arms.

"Pa!" he exclaimed, in a voice that again sounded unnervingly like Tryg's, as he thudded his fist against Tryg's back. "Ach, what's this? Your new woman, and *Pabbi*?"

Tryg squeezed the orc tight, rocking him back and forth, and then drew backward, enthusiastically waving him and the second orc inside. And now that Lydia could see them both properly, she realized that the first orc—the one who'd called Tryg *Pa*—was most certainly his son Tryggr. He had the same tall, lean body, the same quick confident grin, and his long black hair was even tied up into the same messy knot on his head. While the second orc—who was shorter, slimmer, and exceedingly handsome—looked far neater, and also far less sure of himself. His tunic and trousers were perfectly fitted, his hair pulled into a tight braid, and he was biting his lip, and fingering uncertainly at the thick gold choker around his neck.

"Ach, but first we must meet," Tryg said firmly, slinging his long arm around his son's neck, and drawing him forward. "Son, this is our sweet new woman, Lydia, who's brought us great joy this Yule. And woman, this is m'boy Tryggr, the wisest young Skai you'll ever meet! An' this is his sweet clever mate, Eben, of Clan Ka-esh."

This Eben was still looking unmistakably self-conscious, but Tryggr had pulled him close too, pressing a kiss to the top of his head. "The sweetest," he said, with a swift, affectionate grin down toward him, before lurching forward again, toward—Ezog? But yes, yes, this Tryggr was throwing his arms around Ezog too, rocking him back and forth, and Ezog was folding him close, as a slow smile spread across his mouth.

"Happy Yule, son," Ezog said, husky. "We are honoured to welcome you both, ach?"

Lydia was still blinking at all this—Ezog called Tryggr *son*, too?—and Tryggr was easily grinning as he drew away again, his fist bumping Ezog's back. "You too, *Pabbi*," he said brightly, as his dancing eyes flicked toward Lydia. "An' you, woman! I've long wondered what Pa was about with you, but I ken I mostly follow now, ach?"

Lydia was again feeling decidedly lost, but she couldn't help smiling warmly back at this Tryggr anyway. "I'm so happy to finally meet you," she said, without even a hitch in her voice. "I've heard so much about you."

Tryggr kept grinning toward her, his head shaking, his eyes alight. "Ach, wish I could say the same, woman," he said cheerfully, "but Pa's refused to say a word about you! Knew he was up to some sorta old Skai trickery, ach?"

He raised an imperious brow at Tryg, and to Lydia's

surprise, Tryg was actually looking a little sheepish, and waving them toward the table. "Feast first," he said, "and then tales, ach?"

Soon they were all seated around the small table, which turned out to only have three chairs—but Tryggr only pulled Eben down onto his lap, and Lydia somehow found herself settled onto Ezog's, too. While Tryg doled out generous portions of steaming, succulent-smelling breakfast, and poured them multiple mugs of ale and cider.

"So what's the tale, Pa?" Tryggr demanded, once they'd all begun tucking in. "You ken if you don't tell me, I'll get it all outta *Pabbi* later, so out with it, ach?"

He'd shot a teasing grin over toward Ezog as he'd spoken, and suddenly Lydia could easily see Ezog as the soft-hearted, perpetually indulgent father figure, who would willingly give Tryggr whatever he wished. While Tryg himself would no doubt be a far more demanding father, but surely a highly entertaining one, too.

"Ach, ach," Tryg replied, with a rueful grin, as he tossed a whole mushroom into his mouth. "Remembered this old Skai way my own *pabbi* spoke of. How at Yule, Skai-kesh will oft bless a gift, if it's made freely."

Oh. Wait. Because that was new too, wasn't it? And Lydia's searching glance at Ezog behind her found him looking both exasperated and indulgent, his eyes glimmering on Tryg's face. And in return, Tryg reached over and clasped Ezog's knee beneath the table, giving it a companionable little shake. "I've had the worst luck, finding a good woman to share with my sweet *elskan*," he continued, with a grimace. "But I knew he yet longed for this, so I went to Skai-kesh, one last time, and prayed and prayed upon this. And then I went hunting... and found *you*, woman."

His eyes angled toward Lydia, glinting with warmth and

approval. "She was perfect, ach?" he said, his voice lowering. "Soft, and sweet, and kind, and eager to work and gain my praise. Just as my *elskan*. Just as most pleases me."

Tryggr cast a brief, appreciative glance across the table toward Lydia, before pulling Eben a little closer on his lap. "Ach, me also," he replied. "And so?"

"So I tested her, and sought not to hope," Tryg said, with a wincing grimace. "Sought not to oft speak of her, not even to my sweet *elskan*, for I didn't wish to raise his hopes either, ach? But I could taste his sadness upon this, his longing to please me. And so, I asked him to be my Yule gift to her, in hopes of gaining Skai-kesh's blessing. And this was a good test for her also, ach? Catch her by surprise, you ken, so she could not speak false, or seek to trick me."

At that, Tryggr groaned aloud, and without warning, his fist snapped out, and punched Tryg in the arm. "You old weasel, Pa!" he said, with genuine heat in his voice. "*Pabbi*, you oughta tossed him out over this! Gone and found yourself a sweet pretty Ka-esh instead!"

He'd buried his face in Eben's hair, as if drawing much-needed strength from his scent—but behind Lydia, Ezog was smiling again, and shaking his head. "Ach, it has been a long time for your blood-father and I, son," he said softly. "I trust my Skai and his father-god, ach? I ken they shall always care for me."

Tryggr was still sputtering, and jabbing a sharp finger toward his father. "You're damned lucky it worked out, Pa," he said flatly. "It would've served you right, to lose both of 'em. To each other, mayhap."

He shot a sudden, suspicious look toward Lydia and Ezog, and then back at Tryg again. "You get 'em to swear vows to you, at least?" he demanded. "You claim them, and do it all properly?"

Tryg's silver brows had deeply furrowed, his eyes glancing back toward Lydia and Ezog. "I have been... remiss, in swearing vows to my *elskan*," he murmured. "But I hope, mayhap, I have now gained this, with a good long rut upon 'em both, all this Yule's Eve. Must speak to Boss, and then our Enforcer, and Skai-kesh."

Lydia wasn't following again, but behind her, Ezog's body had suddenly gone rigid—and when she glanced toward him, he was staring at Tryg, unblinking, unmoving. And Tryg was half-smiling back, slow and soft and uncertain, but a little hopeful, too.

"Wish to keep you both, for the rest of my days," he said softly. "Wish to grant you all my fealty and care, so long as you both wish for this. Ach?"

Behind Lydia, Ezog twitched again, and he abruptly reached out to clasp Tryg's hand, squeezing it in his own. And then he clasped Lydia's, too, and with firm, gentle pressure, he brought it to his mouth.

"Then I shall also pledge you my troth," he murmured, his voice low and reverent. "To you, Sigtryggr of Clan Skai, and you, Lydia of Clan Bautul. I shall keep you safe, and fed, and filled, for as long as I am able, and as long as you shall wish."

Oh. The words seemed to ripple all through Lydia, resonating up her spine, and Tryg looked just as stunned as she felt, his eyes shimmering on Ezog's face.

"Truly, *elskan*?" he said, disbelieving, almost shy. "Ach. You are—*ach*."

He was rubbing at his face with both hands, and Lydia belatedly realized that his eyes were rapidly blinking, because he was—weeping. Confident, certain, swaggering Tryg was *weeping*, shaking his head, wiping at his eyes.

"Ach," he whispered, his breath oddly gulping. "Ach, *elskan*. I wish for always."

And Lydia was nodding too, silent but fervent, pressing herself into Ezog's safety, his certainty, his great, generous kindness. And in return he was drawing her closer, too, granting her even more of it, of him, as his hand clasped Tryg's again, giving it a gentle, familiar shake.

"Ach, then," he said. "It is settled, I ken."

Settled. Just as he'd said to Lydia earlier, and suddenly she was grinning back and forth between them, while Tryg again wiped at his eyes, and Ezog's own smile split his face. And Lydia only belatedly remembered Tryggr and Eben, watching from across the table—but Eben was looking softly indulgent, and Tryggr appeared distinctly mollified, too.

"Well, about time, Pa," he said flatly, as he plucked up a mushroom with his claws. "Leave it to you to wait 'till you're both *ancient*, honestly."

Tryg spluttered, looking deeply offended, while Ezog huffed a low laugh, and began pouring out more cider. "Now, back to breakfast," he said firmly. "And the rest of the gifts, ach?"

This proved an adequate distraction, and soon they were all happily eating again, and exclaiming over the gifts Ezog had brought. This included a second deadly throwing-knife for Tryggr—who hurled it around the cabin with the same delighted glee Tryg had shown—as well as a complex-looking book of human medical treatments for Eben, who accepted it with surprising eagerness, and then immediately began reading at the table. And then, to Lydia's ongoing astonishment, Ezog presented her with a stunning silver necklace, with a flashing blue jewel attached.

"A sapphire," he murmured at her, "to match your pretty eyes, ach?"

Oh. Oh, gods. Because Ezog hadn't even seen her eyes before this, he would have only known what Tryg had told him—and he'd still gone and bought his partner's mistress a gift? Truly?

"You are too good," Lydia choked, as she threw her arms around him, and buried her face in his neck. "Too good for all of us, *elskan.*"

He shook his head, but drew her close too, enfolding her in his strong warm safety. Holding her there until Tryg came over too, circling his arms around them both, his breaths slightly sniffling into their hair.

But after that, it was easier to get up again, and to join Tryggr and Eben by the fire, drinking more cider, and snacking on plums and sweet breads. And then, at Ezog's suggestion, they each told their favourite Yuletide tale. Tryggr's was one with his Pa and *Pabbi*, in which they'd given him his first dagger, and taught him how to use it— and Eben's was one with his own father, who'd gained him honey for a special Yule treat. While Ezog's tale was one from his youth, when he'd danced with his clan around a faraway altar, and Tryg's was the first Yule he'd spent with his tiny namesake son, rocking him to sleep by a quiet, crackling fire.

And then all four orcs looked at Lydia, waiting for her own tale—and she gave them a wavering smile, and a jerky shrug. "This one," she said thickly. "This one, here, with all of you."

At that, Ezog drew her close again, his arms curling even tighter around her—and then, in another surprise, he began to sing. An old, vaguely familiar carol, sounding strangely deep and haunting in his rich, resonant voice.

But soon the rest of them had joined in, too, Tryg and Tryggr's voices blending almost as one, and finally Lydia sang along too, her voice rising light and clear above them all. And it was such a lovely, homey, shimmering feeling, and once they finished, they sang another carol, and another. Not all of them were ones Lydia knew, but it was easy enough to pick up the melodies, even if she didn't know the words. Easy to sink into the warmth and the cider and the song, into the scents of the firs and the fire, into the strong safety of Ezog's solid arms around her.

Tryggr and Eben finally went to leave once the sun began lowering in the sky, and after a thorough round of hugs and farewells, Lydia was again left alone with Tryg and Ezog. Who promptly spread her out upon the bed, and then took long, luxurious turns with her, kissing her, biting her, filling her with their seed.

And in between rounds, they ate and drank, and sang more songs, and told more tales. Tryg told her about the first night he'd spent with Ezog, how he'd been so dazzled afterwards he'd walked straight into a stone wall. And Ezog told her of the time he'd nearly been killed in a particularly harrowing battle, several years before—and how Tryg had gone to the mountain's powerful young new captain, and held a dagger to his throat until he'd sworn never to send Ezog out again.

And then, perhaps to lighten the darkness of that tale, Ezog told Lydia how he'd helped a constantly exasperated Tryg in dealing with his wild little Skai son, chasing him all about the mountain, while Tryg had punched out his frustrations in the Skai arena. Until Ezog had earned his place as Tryggr's *Pabbi*—the Skai term for a second father—and thereby embedded himself even deeper into Tryg's life, and his heart.

"Knew after that I'd never let you go, *elskan*," Tryg murmured, as his hand easily stroked up and down Ezog's half-hard shaft, his mouth nibbling at his neck. "Too sweet. Too perfect."

Ezog's eyes were fluttering, his breath exhaling in a contented little sigh, and Tryg angled a commanding glance toward Lydia, and then down at Ezog's now-hard cock. And she willingly slipped down to kiss at it, following Tryg's heated directions until Ezog bucked and groaned, and poured out into her mouth.

He tasted different than Tryg did, but still surprisingly sweet, and afterwards Tryg kissed her long and deep, clearly revelling in Ezog's taste on her mouth. And then it was back to sharing more tales and drinks and sweets, sprawling in a messy tangle on the bed, and Lydia even told them, her voice halting, about her husband Tom. About how she'd cared for him so deeply, and grieved him for so long, and then had awoken one day to find herself so utterly, achingly alone.

"Poor little pet," Tryg murmured, tucking her close beneath his arm, as he purposefully tugged Ezog on top of her, and guided her legs apart. "I ken that tiny house of yours was no help, ach? Kept you all cramped and lonesome thus."

As Tryg had spoken, Ezog had again slid himself deep inside her, as if in some sort of comfort—and in truth, it *was* comforting to have him sunk there, to feel him filling all her emptiness, warm and eager and alive. "Ach," he agreed as he began thrusting, his voice hitching with his movements. "You shall thus now come with us. To our home."

Wait. Their home was *Orc Mountain*—but Lydia's lurch of alarm at this recollection was swiftly swept away by Ezog's steady, reassuring presence, by the pleasure and heat swirling from his every powerful thrust inside her. And, too, by the feel of Tryg's soft kiss to her head, his arm firmly pulling her closer.

"Ach, sweet thing," he said, as his other hand clasped to Ezog's shoulder. "My *elskan* speaks truth. We cannot now leave you alone in that house. But should you come to our home, we'll keep you safe, and help you gain work that pleases you. And m'boy and his mate are there too, ach?"

His tone was light and smooth, but there was a clipped, decisive edge on it, as well. As if he would bear no argument on this, and if Lydia even made an attempt, he would...

"You ken what shall come to pass, my pretty pet," came his silken voice, "should you seek to defy me upon this? Have you forgotten whose *elskan* is now deep inside you?"

And oh, that threat was already far more compelling than any unease Lydia had ever felt about Orc Mountain— and a hungry, desperate shiver rippled her from the inside out, convulsing her against Ezog's sweet, gentle invasion. And yes, Ezog felt it, his eyes fluttering hard as they glanced toward Tryg, as if seeking his permission, too...

"I ken she needs a reminder, then," Tryg said smugly, and Lydia's glance up found him slowly grinning between them, sharp and sly and wicked. "Plough your new gift for me, ach, *elskan*? Make her beg and scream for us. Teach her that she shall obey us, and come with us to our home as we wish. For she is *ours*."

And this time, Ezog's smile was just as wicked, lighting up his dear, beautiful face. His eyes catching on Lydia's own slowly widening grin, sharing her eagerness, her thankfulness. Her great, great gratitude, for such a perfect, generous gift. For a home.

"Ach, I shall," Ezog whispered. "With joy."

EPILOGUE

It was almost Yuletide at Orc Mountain, and Lydia truly could not have fathomed just how many preparations were involved.

"Did you say *twelve hundred* cookies?!" she echoed toward Alma, Orc Mountain's kind, pretty head housekeeper. "As in, more than a thousand?!"

Beside Lydia, her silver-haired friend Olga was loudly snorting, and folding her arms over her chest. "I ken you'll still run outta cookies with twelve hundred, sister," she said flatly. "Ain't you seen how much those orclings eat?! Pains me to say, but better make it fifteen."

Alma was wringing her hands and looking distinctly distressed, glancing around at the kitchen's already-packed storeroom. "But we only ordered enough flour for twelve hundred!" she replied. "And it's too late to ship in more, unless we can send someone to..."

She winced and chewed at her lip, and just then, a familiar head poked around the nearest stack of barrels. "Who needs to go where, now?" Tryggr said cheerfully. "To a market again, I ken?"

Alma and Lydia both gave Tryggr deeply grateful smiles, while Olga had already turned to scribble some quantities—and then a few more items—onto a scrap of paper. "Here, boy," she said firmly. "We'll need 'em by morning."

Thankfully, Tryggr was well accustomed to being summarily ordered about, because he only flashed them a tolerant grin, and tossed a nearby cookie—one from Olga's test batch—into his mouth. And when Olga attempted to whack him with her wooden spoon in retaliation, he easily slithered out of her reach, and then snatched a second cookie before speeding away again.

Lydia chuckled, but then quickly went out after him, and caught up with him in the corridor. "Are you sure you don't mind going, Tryggr?" she asked him, as she handed over a third cookie she'd swiped for him, too. "I know you promised Eben no more scouting trips before Yule."

Tryggr's eyes brightened at the new cookie—he'd clearly already devoured the first two—and he shot Lydia an appreciative half-grin as he tossed it into his mouth. "Ach, but then m'pet let it slip there's this new book he wishes to have," he replied, once he'd swallowed. "For this new *Reading Day* the Ka-esh have thrust upon us, the day after Yule! A *whole day* for reading, *Mammi*! I shall be bored enough to weep!"

Lydia laughed aloud, and fought to ignore the sparkle of warmth in her belly at his use of that wonderful word *mammi*. It was the Skai equivalent to *pabbi*, she'd learned, and even after a year, she still hadn't gotten used to Tryggr saying it. Despite him repeatedly pointing out that she was apparently the exact female version of Ezog, from her excessive generosity down to the way she smelled.

"Leave it to Pa," he'd told her one day, with a wry shake of his head. "Can't fathom how long he musta hunted to find a perfect match for *Pabbi*. Like a Grisk on a scent, he is, once he's got an idea stuck in his thick head."

Of course, Tryggr was just as stubborn himself—their similarities were a great source of ongoing amusement for Lydia and Ezog both—and over the past year, Lydia had happily joined Ezog in doting upon Tryggr at every possible opportunity. Sneaking him treats and snacks, cheering on his sparring-matches in the Skai arena, and keeping a close eye on Eben whenever Tryggr was off scouting or working.

"But you and *Pabbi* will send for me if aught's amiss with my sweet pet, ach?" Tryggr said now, his brow furrowing. "An' you won't mind if Pa comes along with me too? Just overnight, I ken."

Lydia smiled and waved away the question, because she'd long ago come to terms with Tryg taking off on these kinds of last-minute jobs. He and Tryggr were both integral members of the Skai clan's extensive scouting team—these days, Tryggr reported directly to the Skai clan's Boss himself—and while Lydia had been surprised to learn how often Tryg travelled, it was also something that was clearly important to him, and to his clan. And something he and Tryggr enjoyed sharing together, too.

"I'll pack you both some provisions," Lydia said firmly. "And while you're at the market, maybe you can remind your father about Yule gifts? I know Ezog would enjoy a nice bottle of wine, and perhaps some sweet treats, too."

Tryggr's smile had gone fond, even as he gave a longsuffering roll of his eyes. "Forgot about the gifts again, has he?" he said dryly. "How you two haven't tossed him yet is beyond fathoming, *Mammi*. Ach, I'll remind him."

Lydia laughed and thanked him, and soon found herself back in the kitchen, packing up a large sack of goodies for the two of them to share. And as she worked, she easily chatted with her now-familiar colleagues and friends—not only Olga and Alma, but also Olga's white-haired orc mate Gegnir, and an elderly Skai named Dufnall, who managed most of the laundry.

And it had been another surprise, at first, to discover that Tryg hadn't expected Lydia to immediately start taking over Orc Mountain's laundry. "Ach, Duff's got it well in hand, sweet thing," he'd told her, with a careless shrug. "If that's what you're hankering to do, I ken he'll make room for you, but mayhap you'd rather take on aught a bit different, ach? No need to rush, you ken."

It had been excessively generous, and Lydia had accordingly taken her time, and given it some thought. Noting, in particular, how Ezog spent his own days, now that he'd mostly stepped back from any fighting or travelling. He didn't have a specific assigned job among his Bautul clan, but he spent most of his time in their beautiful, ever-growing garden, out on the south side of the mountain. And when he wasn't working in the garden, he was helping to stock and supply the kitchen, and making sure the common-rooms and sickroom were well stashed with food, too.

"I should be glad to have you join me, should you wish," Ezog had replied when Lydia had asked, giving her his usual soft smile. "I only do not wish to bore you, ach? Or freeze you."

But Lydia hadn't been bored—or cold, once Ezog had supplied her with some warm layers. In truth, it had been wonderful spending most of her days outdoors doing meaningful work, and getting to know their other Bautul clanmates who worked in the garden, too. This included two lovely young women named Stella and Gwyn—Gwyn also served as the mountain's midwife—and a variety of orcs of all ages. And with Ezog's guidance, Lydia had gradually begun to take over the kitchen stocking, too, freeing up Ezog to explore new opportunities for the garden and the mountain's overall food supply. Lately, he'd even begun to look into acquiring livestock, and Lydia loved seeing his eyes light up whenever he spoke of it.

But the best part of all, of course, was just getting to spend her days with Ezog. Eating lunches together, helping each other, and enjoying one another's quiet company. And even sharing their pleasures together whenever they wished, writhing and moaning in the garden's hidden corners until they were both breathless and sated.

That, too, had been something of a surprise at first, because Ezog's appetite for intimacy had proven remarkably insatiable, and often extended to multiple rounds between them each day. But Lydia loved it too, and found herself almost desperately craving the feel of him locked in place inside her. To the point where he would surreptitiously slip himself up inside whenever she sat on his lap, and they'd even begun sleeping like that, with him curled up close behind her, his cock safely tucked in, too. And there was perhaps no better feeling than to wake up to the sensation of him swelling fully to life, opening her up wide—and then gasping in her ear as he emptied out his first load of the day inside her.

"Ach, you are both so greedy, my pretty pets," Tryg would often say, whenever he happened upon them together, or discovered them in the recent aftermath. "So sweet, when you're reeking thus of each other's fresh scents."

He always seemed fondly pleased by this, and would frequently follow it by joining in for a round, and coolly ordering them to please him. But even so, one afternoon when Ezog had been out, Lydia had gathered her courage, and cornered Tryg in their cozy little bedroom.

"Are you—*sure* you don't mind?" she'd asked him, her voice wavering in a way it rarely did anymore. "About Ezog and me? Even if you're not—there?"

But once again, Tryg had given an affectionate grin, and carelessly waved it away. "Ach, no," he said. "Why do you ken I worked so hard to find a good woman for us? He's always longed for this, and I should only be vexed if he *weren't* enjoying my good gift."

Oh. Lydia's shoulders had sagged with relief, even as she'd kept searching Tryg's eyes—and he'd shrugged, and run a hand through his hair. "An' in truth, it vexed me, leaving him here alone so much," he'd continued. "Gotta do my part for the clan, you ken, but hated the taste of his sadness whenever I'd go off working. But"—his eyes had softened—"it's not near so bad now, ach? Brings me joy, and a lot of peace, to know he's got company. Someone else to empty his bollocks, and warm our bed at nights, and keep a close eye on him for me."

Lydia had felt her shoulders relaxing even more, and Tryg had flashed her another jaunty grin. "And I *know* who you both belong to," he'd purred. "And you both know it, too."

He'd proven it that very night, when he'd worked them both over until they'd both been desperately gasping and shouting and begging for him. And afterwards, he'd pulled both their messy bodies close, and given a deep, contented sigh.

"Ach, Skai-kesh has blessed me," he'd murmured, kissing first Ezog's sweaty forehead, and then Lydia's. "Granted me not only a perfect son, but two perfect mates, too. Couldn't ask for more, ach?"

Both Lydia and Ezog had wholeheartedly agreed, and it was a sentiment that had stayed with Lydia ever since. To the point where she'd begun to thank Skai-kesh each day too, as well as the Bautul clan's patron deity, the goddess of the moon. Worshipping her together with Ezog on a consecrated altar in the garden, offering her thanks for such great, generous gifts.

And those gifts felt particularly powerful now, at Lydia's first Yule in Orc Mountain. Which, despite the intensity of the preparations involved, promised to be a truly delightful time, and she'd easily found herself getting caught up in the Yuletide spirit. Secretly acquiring gifts for her loved ones, and helping to decorate the mountain's corridors and common-rooms, and pitching in wherever she was needed in the kitchen.

"Don't suppose you'd help bake some more of these, then?" Olga was asking her now, giving a disgruntled frown down at the decimated batch of cookies. "Now that your boy's gone and gobbled half of what little we got?"

Lydia chuckled and readily agreed, and soon found herself elbow-deep in cookie dough, chatting merrily with Olga and Gegnir. And then taking a brief moment to say goodbye to Tryg, who stopped by to kiss her farewell before he left, the way he always did. And soon Ezog had come by to help too, and they companionably worked until late in the night, baking as many cookies as they possibly could, before collapsing into bed together.

They welcomed Yule's Eve with a sweet, languid round of lovemaking, and then made their way back to the kitchen again. And when Tryg and Tryggr returned with the supplies ahead of schedule, they were both roped into the baking, too—and between them all, by early afternoon, they'd somehow managed to make all fifteen hundred cookies, as well as a variety of delicious-smelling pies, cakes, and puddings. And Alma had mopped at her brow with palpable relief, before being firmly ordered out of the kitchen by one of her own mates, the Skai Boss Drafli himself.

"Ach, he says the rest of us are to wrap it up too," Tryggr gratefully said, once Drafli had sharply signed something toward him, too. "Finally time for some fun, ach?"

Lydia certainly wasn't about to argue, and soon found herself attired in her festive red Yule dress, and accompanying her mates into the bustling, sweet-scented Grisk common-room. It had been set up as the central hub of the Yule celebrations, and it was beautifully decorated with red ribbons, fresh-cut greenery, and conveniently placed mistletoe.

"Come along, my sweets," said Tryg, with a toothy grin toward Lydia and Ezog. "First we eat and greet, and then we dance, ach?"

It was a lovely way to spend an afternoon, eating and laughing and chatting with their many friends and acquaintances. And once things got a little too heated with the dancing, Tryg herded them both off to the Skai common-room, which was full of a far different kind of celebrating. Including—much to Lydia's amusement—the creative use of silken red ribbons, which had apparently been supplied in bulk for the clan's collective celebrations. And predictably, Lydia's amusement soon turned to wild, desperate craving, as Tryg trussed her and Ezog up like a pair of obscene holiday packages, and then casually took turns fucking them with his hungry, beribboned cock.

And for the grand Yule's Eve finale, the Bautul clan hosted a massive feast out in the garden, around a huge blazing bonfire. The delicious meal of roasted meat and vegetables was accompanied by entertainment from the mountain's orclings, who gathered before the fire to act out a tale—the story of Orc Mountain's founders Edom and Akva, and their five sons, who became the five clans of orcs. And by the end of it, Lydia's stomach hurt from laughing, and she eagerly joined in the cheering and stomping, and firmly congratulated the orclings—and their teachers Geva and Rathgarr—on a job well done.

And finally, once the applause had quieted, a band of Ash-Kai drummers set up around the fire. And against a low, steady drumbeat, all the gathered revellers began to sing together, their rich chorus of voices rising to the clear, moonlit sky.

"That was wonderful," Lydia said afterwards, as she contentedly settled into bed between Ezog and Tryg. "I can't imagine a lovelier way to spend—ack!"

She'd been tackled by a devious-looking Tryg, who was glaring down at her with mock disbelief. "Ach, what is this?" he demanded at her. "Have you yet forgotten the perfect Yule's Eve I granted you last year? I ken you need a reminder, my greedy little pet."

It led to yet more delightful Yule's Eve fun, with Tryg ordering Ezog to have his hungry way with Lydia, until he finally joined in, too. And by the end of it, they were all a sore, exhausted, sticky mess, but Lydia couldn't stop smiling as she kissed them both goodnight. And then she slipped into a soft, easy sleep, tucked in her usual place in Ezog's strong safe arms.

"It is Yule, my sleepy pets!" Tryg announced bright and early the next morning, as he dragged in a steaming bath, and then plunked a basket of sweets onto Ezog's belly. "Now bathe, and eat, and then gifts, ach?"

His enthusiasm was contagious, and soon they were all

up and freshly bathed, and exclaiming over their gifts. Tryg had gotten both Lydia and Ezog a variety of human-made wines and snacks—surely from his trip to the market the day before—but to their mutual delight, he'd also acquired them a selection of rare seeds for the garden, too. While Ezog gave Tryg another new weapon—a throwing-spear— and for Lydia, he'd ordered a beautiful set of sturdy, perfectly fitted boots and gloves, meant to help keep her warm in the garden.

Lydia had agonized for weeks over what to give them both, but after consulting with Olga and Alma—who both knew quite a lot about orc gifting traditions—she'd settled on jewels. On a thick gleaming cuff for Ezog, with sapphires that matched the pendant he'd given her the year before. And for Tryg, a sleek, deadly dagger for his hair, with more blue sapphires studded halfway down. Ensuring that the jewels would be hidden by his hair when worn, preventing the possibility of some secret scouting position being betrayed by unexpected glittering.

"Did you have Argarr make this, pet?" Tryg delightedly demanded, once he'd unwrapped it. "Ach, this is so *thoughtful*, my sweet!"

Lydia fondly grinned as he promptly unwound his long silver hair from its current dagger, and then wrapped his new one into it, tilting his head back and forth. "And so light, too!" he continued brightly. "Ach, it is perfect. Thank you, pet. Both of you. I am so blessed, this Yule."

He'd yanked both her and Ezog close, and Lydia happily squeezed him back, blinking away the sudden prickling wetness behind her eyes. Because truly, it still felt almost impossible that this kind of happiness could be hers. That she was safe and warm at home, celebrating Yule with the people she loved most.

But the warmth only shimmered higher as they launched into another full day of Yule celebrations, even more marvellous than the day before. Beginning with more gift exchanging with Tryggr and Eben—more weapons for Tryggr, and books for Eben—and then a delicious breakfast, hosted by the Ash-Kai clan this time.

And then, for Yule itself, it turned out that each clan held a specific activity to celebrate, and all other clan members were welcome to join in. It began with a Grisk cookie-decorating event, which was enthusiastically attended by dozens of excitedly squealing orclings—who, as Olga had expected, each seemed to consume their own body weight in cookies. It was followed by a cheery Ash-Kai morning of tales in the schoolroom, and then a clever Ka-esh crafting session—which was again heavily attended by enthusiastic orclings, who soon were eagerly flying little paper birds and dragons throughout the mountain's corridors.

Next was a Bautul project that Lydia and Ezog had helped to organize—an intensive gift hunt, in which teams of searchers raced to seek out hidden little gifts, which were each destined for a specific recipient. It led to a wild afternoon of orcs racing and shouting and laughing all through the mountain, and it turned out that Tryg was one of the top performers, single-handedly delivering no fewer than a dozen gifts to their intended recipients.

And finally, for the main event of the day, the Skai clan hosted a massive sparring tournament in the Skai arena. Teaming up pairs of fighters from across all five clans, while hundreds of spectators shouted and cursed and cheered from the rows of surrounding stone seats. Unsurprisingly, the Skai made an excellent showing—Tryggr very high among them—and even Tryg made it through multiple rounds before conceding defeat to a sturdy Grisk named Varinn.

"A few decades back, I'd have flattened him," Tryg told Lydia and Ezog with a resigned grin, rubbing a hand at his sweaty face. "But I'll take great joy in seeing m'boy do it, ach?"

It turned out that Tryggr did indeed defeat Varinn, but it was a close thing, helped greatly by a stunning sideways kick that was perfectly suited to his lean, quick body. "Learnt that from me, he did," Tryg proudly told Lydia, in between bouts of ear-splitting cheering. "That's m'boy! Get him, son!"

In the end, Tryggr was just edged out by an equally slim and speedy Ka-esh, a development that left Tryg highly indignant. "A Ka-esh, son?" he demanded once a sweaty Tryggr had come to sprawl beside them, with a flush-faced Eben in tow. "What rubbish is this?!"

"Ach, I'd like to see you try an' take him, Pa," Tryggr said, between heaving breaths, as he bodily yanked Eben onto his lap. "These Ka-esh have got more surprises than you think, ach?"

He was already nuzzling at Eben's neck, making him wriggle and gasp, while Tryg pursed his lips, and shook his head. "Ach, I follow, son," he said flatly. "Don't want to stomp a pretty Ka-esh in the face, not when you're so smitten with your own! I ken you oughta—"

But before he could finish, Ezog had moved to drop his huge body in between Tryg and Tryggr, elbowing Tryg powerfully in the side. "This was a fine showing, son," he said firmly. "You were a joy to watch, ach?"

Thankfully Tryg took the hint, though he kept casting dark looks over toward Tryggr and Eben—at least, until Ulfarr, another Skai, knocked out his equally massive

Bautul opponent with a spectacular punch to the head. A development that led to more shouting and cheering, especially since the tournament was down to only four final contestants—three of them Skai, with one lone Ash-Kai remaining.

Even Lydia could admit that the final two matches were very exciting, and the contestants were clearly taking their time now, and putting on a good show for their rapt audience. But finally, two more winners were announced—one of them the Skai Boss Drafli, the other one his gigantic clan brother Simon. And their final match was a stunning display of skill and speed and strength, which ended with the two of them clasping hands, and then collapsing down onto the floor together.

The cheering afterwards was so loud it shook the room, and soon the party spilled out into the corridor, which had been well stocked with cakes, eggnog, and the last of the cookies. And by the end of it, Lydia felt giddy and dizzy and utterly exhausted, and she was deeply grateful when Ezog finally guided her back toward their room, with Tryg close behind.

"Ach, that's it," Tryg murmured, his voice husky and warm, as Ezog pulled up Lydia's red dress, and sank himself deep inside her. "Give her a good hard Yule ploughing with that perfect fat prick of yours, *elskan*. Make her scream and plead for my good gift, ach?"

And yes, yes, Ezog was already doing it, plunging in with long, powerful strokes, while Lydia gasped and clung to him, welcoming him, pleading for him. Telling him what a good, wonderful gift he was, how much she loved having him inside her, making her his own.

And when Tryg climbed up behind him, strengthening Ezog's deep plunges with his own vicious thrusts, she begged for him too, praising him, adoring him. "You're so generous, Tryg," she choked at him. "So giving. So, so good to me. To us."

And gods, the way he grinned at her, bright and wicked and approving, flashing her all those sharp teeth. "Ach, no," he said, his voice hitching as he slammed inside, wringing the desperate craving up higher, harder. "Just greedy, you ken. Wanting to keep my perfect sweet gifts all to myself, for all the rest of our Yules together."

Oh. And even as Lydia arched and shouted with pleasure, with the truth of two orcs pouring themselves out as one, those words kept ringing, thudding like a deep, quiet bell. *Greedy. To keep my perfect sweet gifts all to myself.*

And when Tryg collapsed down onto Ezog's broad, sweaty back, she ran her hands down his sides, and searched his eyes. Finding that rare twinge of vulnerability, or maybe even shame. An admission, perhaps, that he needed them too, just as much as they needed him. That in giving them both such great gifts, he'd also been giving them to... himself.

"Good," Lydia told him, quiet but certain. "Because we're all yours, Tryg, always. For all the Yules we have left, and all the days in between."

And Tryg was half-smiling back at her, still looking surprisingly vulnerable, almost a little shy. "Ach?" he said, quiet. "You ken?"

Lydia firmly nodded, giving him a shy, wavering smile of her own. "I ken," she whispered. "I swear, Tryg."

Above her, Ezog was nodding too, and even nudging his neck closer to Tryg's mouth. And that was another bright, impish, contagious grin, lighting up Tryg's face—and without another word, he bent his head to his *elskan*'s waiting neck, and bit his teeth deep.

BONUS EPILOGUE

It was two days before Yule, and Lydia didn't have a gift for Tryg.

"What do you mean, Argarr didn't finish the dagger?" she demanded at her heart-son Tryggr, her voice shrill. "Why in the gods' names not? He told me it was nearly done three days ago!"

Tryggr shot her a wry, regretful grimace, shaking his head. "Came down with a nasty infection, I ken," he said. "M'pet says it was from some travelling human salesman buying some blades. Efterar's ordered 'em both into one of the Skai lodges, until they clear the thing. Sounds like it's a tricky one to fully heal, and he don't want to risk an outbreak right on Yule."

Lydia wrinkled her nose and sighed, the dismay still twisting in her belly. "And there's no way for someone else to finish the dagger in time?" she asked. "Just... polish it up a little, or something?"

But Tryggr gasped with genuine-seeming horror, whipping his head back and forth. "Ach, no!" he exclaimed.

"T'was made to match Pa's other one, ach? You can't have someone else mucking round with Argarr's work! Skai-kesh forbid, they'd ruin it! Poor Pa would have a fainting attack!"

He sounded deeply scandalized, and Lydia sighed again, her shoulders heavily slumping. "But now I don't have a gift for your father," she said helplessly. "And the Grisk Shop is closed for Yule, and it's too late for me to travel anywhere, and all our baking was for the celebrations—and my gift for Ezog isn't at all something that can be shared! And it isn't only Yule, but also our anniversary! Oh, what am I going to do?!"

Her voice had gone shrill, almost panicked, her eyes pleading on Tryggr's face. To which he only gave her a fond, reassuring smile, and clasped her on the shoulder. "Look, Pa don't care, *Mammi,*" he said, quiet but firm. "He'll understand, ach? You ken he'll be glad to have the dagger when it's ready. And he'll be thankful you didn't hand it off to some fool hack of a smith, either."

His eyes darkened again at even the thought of it, and Lydia fought to steady her breaths, to attempt some semblance of a nod. Prompting Tryggr to give her a gentle shake, his smile gone even more tolerant than before. "I can smell you, *Mammi,*" he said. "Don't you worry yourself about it. You ken it's not those kinds of gifts Pa really wants at Yule anyway, ach?"

Lydia blinked at him, not following, and Tryggr gave a cheerful roll of his eyes, together with another little shake to Lydia's shoulder. "Pa wants *you, Mammi,*" he said. "You, an' *Pabbi.* Ach?"

Oh. Lydia kept blinking uncertainly toward him, but her breaths were coming deeper again, her heartbeat slowing in her chest. While Tryggr flashed her another jaunty, reassuring grin, before spinning around, and striding down the corridor in the direction of the Ka-esh wing. "Just let us know if we can help," he called over his shoulder, "but I don't want to see any of it, for the love of Skai-kesh."

Lydia choked a laugh and shook her head, but once Tryggr's tall form had disappeared around the corner, she felt her head tilting, her brow furrowing. *It's not those kinds of gifts Pa really wants.* And now Lydia's memories were casting backwards, to their first Yule together, three years before. To when Tryg had told her not to bring a gift, and had then turned around and given her Ezog, tied in a red bow.

In retrospect, it had been so typical of Tryg, just the kind of thing he so often did. Dismissing his own gifts, his own needs, in favour of focusing on the people he cared about. And it was part of why Lydia had always gone out of her way to pick out thoughtful gifts for him, to remind him that he was loved, and valued, and appreciated. That she and Ezog would never stop caring for him, just as Tryg cared for them. That they were his, always his, for all the Yules they had left.

But amidst that, Lydia had perhaps lost sight of the truth of that first gift. The deep, powerful meaning of it. The way it hadn't been about material things whatsoever, but instead, just about... them. Their love, their trust, their joy together.

Lydia's thoughts were spinning, now, her heart racing in her chest, and she took off down the corridor, in the direc-tion of the gardens. Toward where she knew Ezog was hard at work, helping their Bautul clan prepare for the Yule's Eve feast—but upon catching scent of her at the garden's entrance, Ezog instantly came over to greet her, his beloved face creased with concern.

"What is it?" he asked, drawing her close into his warm strong arms. "Is aught amiss? Are you unwell?"

Lydia was already relaxing into Ezog's solid, familiar

reassurance, her breath hitching as she exhaled. "I need a new gift for Tryg," she said, muffled, into his chest. "Will you help me give him something special?"

She already knew Ezog's answer, even before he spoke it, but it was more comfort, more reassurance, to see his warm, willing smile, the eager approval kindling in his eyes. Almost as if... as if he'd somehow been waiting for her to ask.

"Ach, my sweet," he said. "I should be most honoured."

THE NEXT EVENING found Lydia pacing back and forth in the cozy, familiar Skai cabin, waiting for Tryg to arrive.

The cabin was all ready for Yule, with a cheerful fire crackling in the fireplace, a pile of gifts and treats on the table, and multiple boughs of fresh-cut spruce and fir on the mantel. But most important of all was Lydia's gift, sitting wrapped on the bed in a red silk robe, and smiling fondly toward her.

"There is no need to fret, my sweet," Ezog said, his voice low and reassuring. "You ken Tryg should be pleased with aught you gave him, ach?"

Lydia nodded and shot Ezog a distracted, grateful smile back, even as she kept pacing. "Yes, I know," she said thickly, "but that's just the problem! He's always pleased with everything, and never asks for anything, when he gives me so much. And I just"—she drew in breath, her voice wavering—"I want him to know, to really, really know, how much I—"

She froze at the sound of a brisk rap on the door, her eyes wide on Ezog's face—but he kept smiling as he rose to his feet, pressed a gentle kiss to her hair, and nudged her toward the door. "He knows," he said. "We both do, ach?"

Lydia's smile back felt weepy this time, but she nodded, and lurched over to the door. Yanking it open, and finding a tall, broadly grinning Tryg waiting behind it, with a sack slung over his shoulder. "There you are, sweet thing," he said brightly, as he bent down for a kiss, and strode past her into the cabin. "Now, what are you two getting up to out—"

But his voice broke there, because his gaze had caught on Ezog, now standing in the middle of the cozy, firelit room. And Lydia was looking at Ezog too, her breath exhaling shaky and slow as she glanced up and down, seeing him with fresh, appreciative eyes.

He was... resplendent. Not only due to his silk red robe—borrowed from their similarly-sized Grisk friend Eyarl—but also with his long glossy hair, his gleaming, freshly oiled skin, and the gold jewels glittering on his wrists, his fingers, his ears. All of the jewels gifts from Lydia—and Tryg—over the past few years, because it had turned out that Ezog was shyly delighted by jewels, and took great joy in adorning himself for his mates.

Never woulda guessed it, sweet thing, Tryg had gratefully told Lydia, the day after Ezog had wept upon receiving a beautifully forged gold ring, with the traditional Skai vow of matehood engraved inside it. *Looks good in jewels, though, doesn't he?*

Ezog did look good in jewels, Lydia could readily admit, especially in strong, heavy pieces that shone and glittered against his big scarred body, somehow drawing out his rugged, unearthly beauty even more than before. And in this moment, Tryg looked genuinely struck by the sight of it, his eyes glinting with appreciative admiration as they flicked up and down Ezog's robed form.

"Very pretty, *elskan*," he said, his voice hoarse, before his gaze darted back to Lydia. "An' you too, sweet thing."

Lydia was clad in her usual red Yule dress, of course, along with some of her own lovely jewels—a bracelet, earrings, her matching rings from Tryg and Ezog—but she waved it away, and clasped Tryg's hand in hers. "I wanted to give you something special for Yule," she said, her heart still skipping unevenly in her chest. "So I thought you might appreciate... this."

Tryg's silver brows snapped up, his gaze gone rather bemused as it swept back to Ezog again. "Ach, always, sweet thing," he said lightly. "Looks good in red, doesn't he?"

Lydia choked a strangled, nervous laugh, her face heating. "I mean... *Ezog* is your—your Yule gift," she said, with a helpless wave toward him. "So you need to—unwrap him."

The comprehension instantly passed across Tryg's eyes, a low chuckle huffing from his throat. "Ach, now I see," he said, angling a quick, conspiratorial glance toward Lydia. "Returning the favour, are you?"

Lydia rapidly, gratefully nodded, and Tryg's smile grew into something hungry and wolfish as he gave her arse a gentle little slap, and prowled closer toward Ezog. Toward where Ezog was still standing immobile in his red robe, his mouth softly smiling, his face deeply flushed. And Lydia could see Tryg now taking in the way Ezog was standing, rather more stiffly than usual, with a very obvious tent at the front of his robe.

"Well, look at this," Tryg said, clearly already warming to the game, as he began striding a slow, assessing circle around Ezog's waiting, unmoving body. "I wonder what our sweet woman has wrapped up for me? Something very tasty, I ken."

Ezog's face flushed even redder, and Tryg flashed him a

gleeful grin as he kept circling, now trailing his clawed hand gently over the fabric covering Ezog's chest. "An' something just as pretty on the inside as it is on the outside. Something I'd like to lick all over, and fill up with good Skai frosting."

Ezog's breath audibly caught, his eyes glimmering bright on Tryg's face, and Tryg's smug smile pulled even wider as he halted before Ezog, and tugged at the silken tie clinching the robe closed. "Let's see, then," Tryg purred, slowly drawing out the tie from around Ezog's waist. "What's going to be *mine*, this Yule."

There was a deep, decisive satisfaction in his voice, and then flaring in his eyes, as he yanked the tie fully away, and shoved the robe off Ezog's shoulders. Revealing the full sight of Ezog's bulky body, now slightly shivering in the open air.

And though Lydia knew full well what had been hidden beneath the robe, her breath still caught as she looked, her eyes running up and down. Drinking up the sight of Ezog's big, scarred, familiar form, glinting in yet more of their jewels—but also wrapped in multiple thick red ribbons, at all the most strategic places. Around his neck. Across his collarbones and chest, and over his nipples. Around his waist. And most of all, the ribbons were wound extensively around his groin, making it look almost as though he was wearing a full girdle of red, with a large, highly conspicuous bulge jutting out in front—which, of course, was adorned with an extra red bow.

"Ach," Tryg said, low in his throat, as his eyes shifted between amusement, appreciation, and unmistakable craving. "Wrapped him up real good for me, did you, sweet thing?"

Lydia twitched a nod, and then jerked closer toward Ezog, settling a hand against where—wait—his arm was still trembling, perhaps not only from the cool air. "Such a good gift deserves extra ribbons," she said, as lightly as she could. "Don't you think?"

She'd shot an intent, urgent-feeling smile up at Ezog's face, at where he was indeed looking suddenly—shy. Almost *nervous*. After he'd kept telling her not to fret, and that Tryg would welcome whatever she gave him. But perhaps it was one thing to speak such reassurances, and another to be brazenly gussied up as a Yuletide gift, waiting for a beloved partner's response, and his judgement.

And perhaps—the thought occurred to Lydia, far too late—perhaps this was calling to mind the last time Ezog had been asked to do this, three years before. When Tryg had wanted him to come and be a gift to his mistress, a woman Ezog hadn't even yet met. A situation that had to have been horribly distressing, and yet here Ezog was again, risking this again, for her. For them.

"Don't you think?" Lydia asked again, her voice rising, her eyes now desperately searching Tryg's face. "He's such a good gift, isn't he?"

Because—because Tryg's expression had shifted, too. His amusement fading, sobering, into something quieter, something watchful. Something almost... reverent.

"Ach," Tryg murmured, husky, as his hand found Ezog's chin, caressed gentle against it. "The best, my sweets. An' here I thought my *elskan* could never be more beautiful, ach?"

Oh. The relief shuddered warm and stunning into Lydia's belly, and she could see it flashing across Ezog's face too, softening his blinking eyes. While Tryg's mouth slowly curled back into its smug, satisfied grin, and he stepped a little backwards, licking his lips as he glanced up and down Ezog's red-wrapped body.

"Now, where ought I to begin, sweet thing?" he asked, with a sly glance toward Lydia. "Anywhere I wish?"

Lydia shyly nodded, and watched as Tryg's clever clawed fingers eagerly caught into the ribbon at Ezog's throat, drawing him a little closer. A movement that already had Ezog gasping, and Tryg again licked his lips as he gave it another purposeful yank, his eyes darkening with obvious hunger. "Ach, mayhap we leave that one for now," he purred, keeping one hand tucked into it, while his other hand wandered down to Ezog's chest. To the thick ribbon wrapped around his ribs, fully covering his nipples, which looked—Lydia could admit—unusually, strikingly peaked.

"Ach, what's this?" Tryg breathed, as he unwrapped the ribbon, pulling it downwards, and revealing—gold, glinting at both Ezog's deep green nipples. Not piercings, no, but clever little clips, clasping tightly at Ezog's nipples, and dangling down with short, shining chains of gold.

The clips were something Lydia had remembered Tryggr joking about, once—he'd been teasing Eben about Ka-esh proclivities—and when she'd gathered up her courage the day before to go ask them, it had turned out they'd had an extra set on hand that they'd been willing to donate to the cause.

These ones are too weak anyway, Tryggr had said, with a rueful grin, and a teasing snap of his teeth toward Eben beside him. *You like a bit more bite with your gold, don't you, pet?*

So Lydia had thoroughly cleaned and sterilized the clips, and had shyly shown them to Ezog, who'd only rapidly nodded, his face flushing. And properly clipping them onto his nipples had turned out to be a highly intriguing project, which had ended with Lydia taking a quick, breathless ride on his swollen cock, gently tugging at the clips' chains all the while.

It was a potential that Tryg clearly hadn't missed, trailing the chains through his fingers, his eyes glinting on Ezog's reddened face. And when he gave one of them an experimental little tug, Ezog gasped and shivered all over, his eyes rolling back, his hands clutching to fists at his sides.

"Oh, I *like*," Tryg said now, his voice heated and husky, as he gave another brief, purposeful tug at the chain. "And you like, too, don't you, *elskan*? Like having chains attached to you, for your mates to use as we please?"

Ezog gasped again, nodding, and Tryg's smile curled higher as his hands slid downwards, finding the next ribbon—around Ezog's waist—and swiftly tugging that off, too. Revealing Ezog's taut, familiar belly, but now with something red and white tucked into its navel.

"Candy!" Tryg crowed, as he plucked it out, and tossed it into his mouth. "Ooooh, mint! Just as tasty as you, *elskan*."

Lydia and Ezog both laughed, perhaps a little shaky, and now Lydia took a breath, and grasped for Ezog's bare shoulder. Nudging him to spin around, and he willingly went, showing Tryg his broad, now-bared back. Which instead of ribbons, now sported something new and dark, stamped across his deep green skin.

It was inked script, large and bold, written in a lovely, flowing hand that seemed to ripple across the muscles of his back. And at Ezog's suggestion, it said, *Gifted to Sigtryggr, of Clan Skai.*

The idea had seemed preposterous, at first, but Eben had shyly suggested it during the clip discussion, pointing out that ink-marking mates was an old northern Ka-esh tradition. And after a helpful consultation with Eben's Ka-esh sisters Rosa and Daisy, Lydia had learned that the inks were derived from the flowers of a particular underground plant, and though they weren't permanent, they could last for weeks, or sometimes months, depending on the formulation. And while the northern Ka-esh most often used them for marking their mates, they were apparently also used for sacred purposes, or to bring luck or skill or blessing.

"Rosa had her kin-brother Tristan write the script out on paper for me, because she says he has the best penmanship in the realm," Lydia said now, into the sudden, stilted silence. "And then I did my best to copy it onto Ezog with the ink. Apparently it'll stay like that on him for a week or two, at least."

She'd been speaking too quickly, her face again flushing hot, because gods, what if Tryg laughed. What if he thought it was foolish, or mawkish, or just too much, or...

"Can I touch it?" Tryg asked into the silence, his voice stilted. "Or might that ruin it?"

Lydia cast a sidelong look up at Tryg's face—was he *blushing*?—and nodded, reaching up to stroke her hand over Ezog's warm, ink-marked skin. "No, you're fine to touch it," she said. "Though I'm told if you cut into it, the ink might heal into the cut. So be careful with your claws, if you don't want it staying that way."

But Tryg's tooth was biting his lip as his claw reached up to touch Ezog's back too, tracing gently against the lines of his name. "Pretty, though, ain't it?" he murmured, hushed. "My name looks real nice on you, *elskan*."

That was unmistakably a shiver, quivering through Ezog's shoulders, and in a jerky movement, Tryg bent forward, and pressed his mouth to that marked, inked skin. "Real nice," he breathed, his lashes fluttering, as his hips ground up against Ezog's still-red-wrapped arse. "Will be so sweet to look upon whilst I plough you, ach?"

Ezog visibly shivered again, arching back into where Tryg's claws were already tugging at the ribbon—and Lydia belatedly caught at Tryg's hand, even though her own cheeks were still smarting hot, the heat simmering in her groin. "No ploughing yet," she said, through her constricted throat. "You have to finish unwrapping him first!"

Tryg's glance toward Lydia was wry and a little embarrassed, and he ran a clawed hand through his hair. "Ach, sweet thing," he croaked. "Just a bit dazzled by your good gift, you ken."

Lydia's smile back was bright and delighted, and she swiftly turned Ezog around again, to where he was looking rather stunned, too. The tent beneath his ribbons was jutting out even larger than before, and Tryg huffed a low, groaning laugh as he leaned closer, skating his claws over it with eager, reverent hunger.

"So pretty, *elskan*," he breathed, his eyes hooded on Ezog's face. "So perfect."

Ezog's breath heaved through his chest, his own eyes blinking rapt on Tryg's, and Tryg gave himself a bracing little shake, before angling another wry glance toward Lydia. "You really know how to treat a fella, sweet thing," he murmured, as he carefully reached for the red bow at Ezog's tented groin, and plucked it apart with his claw. "I wonder what you've hidden for me under here? A nice, fat, pretty prize, I ken."

Lydia choked another laugh, even as her eyes stayed fixed on the sight of Tryg unwrapping that thick ribbon, winding it off around Ezog's hips. Unlooping it lower and lower, exposing more and more of Ezog's bare scarred torso, and then—Lydia's breath caught—the fall of silken red, fluttering light and easy from Ezog's hips.

"Ach, is this—*Skai garb*?" Tryg demanded, his voice rising. "Truly?"

He was tearing away the rest of the ribbon, now, letting it fall at Ezog's ankles, and revealing the full sight of the traditional red Skai loincloth beneath. It was slung low and flattering on Ezog's hips, and though its front rectangle of red would usually have fallen down to his thighs, it was currently jutting straight out toward them, draped bright and obscene over Ezog's huge, erect cock beneath.

"Ach, look at that," Tryg said, his voice hushed. "Ach, and it—it matches you, sweet thing! Scents of you!"

He waved wildly at Lydia's red Yule dress, and then hesitated, frowning down at the bottom of it—at where the hem was a good deal higher than it had once been. And Lydia laughed again as she nodded, and gave a gentle caress to the matching fabric draped over Ezog's cock. "We thought it would be nice if we matched, didn't we?" she said lightly. "Thought you might like it, Tryg."

And yes, yes, Tryg did like it, that was clear, and he'd even nudged Lydia over to stand beside Ezog, so he could sweep his glittering eyes up and down them both. "Ach, I like," he purred. "Henceforth, you shall both wear these, for all our Yules."

Lydia easily nodded along with Ezog, and felt his arm slipping around her waist, drawing her closer against his side. While Tryg just kept looking at them, his eyes rapidly blinking, his chest visibly hollowing. "So pretty, my sweets," he breathed. "All you need now is—"

He bit his lip again, shaking his head, and now his hands were fumbling for Ezog's red loincloth, yanking the fabric to the side. And revealing yet another intricate gold gift, one

Lydia hadn't even known about, until Ezog had sheepishly taken her to their room the day before, and pulled it out from beneath his clothes.

"It is called a *typpavír*," he'd said, his face reddening. "The Grisk goldsmiths have begun making them, and I thought—I thought Tryg should be pleased, to see me wear one. So I had—ordered this for us, for Yule."

Oh. It had been Ezog's own gift, for Tryg, and for her. And Lydia had blinked at it, tracing a searching finger against the thick gold ring, much like a large bracelet—but clipped to it were two dangling, glittering chains, leading to a slim gold post, about the size of Lydia's littlest finger.

"That doesn't go on—" Lydia had said, blinking between it, and Ezog's reddened face. "Does it?"

Ezog had swallowed and nodded, looking shyly, adorably mortified, and Lydia had rapidly collected herself, and firmly reassured him that of course Tryg would love it, and that she surely would, too. To which Ezog had gone even redder, even as he'd gratefully smiled toward her, and told her that perhaps it could be a surprise for them both, then.

Which meant that Lydia hadn't fully seen this yet, either, beyond a few glimpses beneath the loincloth as she'd wrapped him in the ribbon. And she now found herself staring at it together with Tryg, as more heat pooled and simmered at her groin.

Because oh, how it looked. Ezog's long, fat, silken green length now adorned, gleaming with gold, like the true prize it was. Gold that began around his base, the thick ring tucked close to his skin beneath his full, softly furred bollocks. And extending from the ring were those glittering chains, leading all the way up his shaft. Until the chains reached his smooth glossy cleft, to where it was visibly opened, stretched, with that slim post of gold buried down inside it.

It was highly shocking, and deeply compelling, too, seeing that familiar beautiful cock propped and pinioned, blatantly on display, just like the rest of him. And Lydia felt almost light-headed, now, with all the blood apparently pooling to her groin at once, while beside her, Tryg was letting out a low, helpless-sounding moan, his gaze frozen on the sight, his clawed hand clutching convulsively at the front of his own tented trousers.

"Look at you, *elskan*," he breathed, his black tongue curling at his lips. "This is... you are..."

He seemed truly lost for words, his tongue licking again and again, and his shaky hand had skittered over to stroke at it, to pluck gently at those taut gold chains. A movement that instantly swayed Ezog on his feet, a hoarse groan growling from his throat, his eyes rolling back—and Tryg's smile was slow, wicked, ravenous, as he did it again, again, again.

"So pretty," Tryg rasped, through heaving breaths, as Ezog trembled and moaned before him. "So perfect, *elskan*."

Lydia had perhaps never seen Ezog's face so flushed, and he shook his head, his eyes wild on Tryg's face. To which Tryg leaned forward, and gave a hard, biting kiss to Ezog's mouth, even as his hand gave a firm little yank at the chain on his nipple. "Perfect," he hissed. "And mine. *Ours*."

Ezog's moan was desperate, helpless, while Tryg's eyes flashed with heated, hungry satisfaction. "And now I'm gonna keep unwrapping you, *elskan*," he purred. "Gonna keep opening you up for me, ach?"

With that, his clever fingers loosened the *typpavír*'s chains, unhooking them from the solid base, so that they dangled from that embedded post of gold. A post that Tryg was now gently tugging, drawing it out slow and certain, his eyes darting rapid and greedy between Ezog's face, and Ezog's impaled, visibly spasming cock.

"Ach, what a gift this is," Tryg breathed, as his chest heavily swelled and hollowed, his fluttering eyes now fixed to the gleaming gold rod slipping out further, and further, and further. "I wonder what it shall grant me when I—"

His voice broke as the gold slipped out, and Lydia caught a glimpse of that soft, opened channel, convulsing on its own—and then spraying out spurt after spurt of thick, messy white. Spewing onto Tryg's hands, his clothes, and with a moan, a frantic flashing drop, Tryg was on his knees, swallowing Ezog's convulsing cock deep into his mouth, gulping that rich sweetness down his moaning, greedy throat.

The sound from Ezog's mouth was almost a roar, one hand frantically grasping for Tryg's head, the other clamping around Lydia's waist, drawing her tightly into his side. So she could join him in this moment, in revelling in the sight and the power of it, in their cool, confident, powerful Tryg brought to his knees by the sheer strength of their good gift.

"You like?" Lydia finally asked, her voice hitching in her throat, once Tryg had stopped swallowing—and for an instant, he only gazed at her, while something sharp and strange shifted in his eyes. Something searching, assessing, waiting for...

His—*attack.* His lean coiled body snapping up, snatching Lydia bodily into his arms, and hurling her onto her back on the bed. And then whipping back around, clawing for Ezog, and shoving him to his knees on the bed before Lydia, his hand tangling deep in Ezog's long, shining hair.

"Feast upon our woman, *elskan*," he growled, hot and commanding, as his other hand flung up Lydia's red dress, and shoved Ezog's face in close. "Reward her for such a good gift. Make her beg and scream upon you, whilst I—"

His voice cracked, faltered, because his hand had swept down, yanking up the red loincloth in the back, too. Revealing Ezog's bare, muscled, deep green arse, now raised high toward him, with just a glint of red ribbon visible between his firm arse-cheeks.

"Whilst I keep opening you," Tryg gasped, hoarse, breathless, as his hand fluttered down to caress at it, to begin drawing out that familiar gold weight—a gift from the year before, but now with a bright red ribbon tied on the end. And oh, the way Tryg looked, sliding it out like that, his eyes worshipful on the sight, while Ezog arched and moaned, and buried his face deeper between Lydia's legs. His tongue trembly and shaky against her slick clutching heat, and Lydia could only gasp and moan and watch, the pleasure swirling, sweeping higher with every breath...

The gold finally escaped Ezog in a slick-sounding squelch, his deep groan vibrating hard into Lydia's swollen, quivering crease. While Tryg blatantly eyed what he'd just opened, his lashes fluttering, his tongue dragging slow and hungry at his lips.

"Look at you, sweet *elskan*," he rasped. "With your sweet rump opened wide and waiting for me, and your sweet tongue buried deep into our sweet woman, bringing her such joy. What a perfect, perfect gift you are."

Ezog's groan was harsh, helpless, but he kept licking, feasting, his tongue curling deep and wondrous inside Lydia, swiping at that perfect place again and again. While Tryg ran a slow, possessive hand up Ezog's inked back, his fingers spreading wide, until they again curled around that red ribbon, still tied around Ezog's throat.

"So sweet," Tryg continued, a low growl in his throat, as he gave the ribbon a gentle tug, making Ezog twitch and shiver all over. "So pretty, with my name on your skin, and my ribbon round your throat. And"—his breath choked as he shifted behind Ezog, lining himself up—"with my strong Skai prick, buried deep in your rump."

He slammed forward sharp and vicious, the sound of slapping skin ringing out between them. And Ezog again quaked beneath it, his tongue's movements shaky and sloppy as Tryg rammed inside again and again. One hand still clutched at that ribbon, yanking Ezog's head back, while his other hand slid around to tug at the swaying chain on his nipple, the touch wrenching Ezog's groans to deep, desperate cries.

"So pretty, *elskan*," Tryg gasped again, his eyes blazing. "And you'll be even prettier once you're ploughing that fat, opened prick into our sweet, lovely woman, ach?"

Oh yes, oh please, and Lydia was nodding just as hard as Ezog, grasping at him, yanking him up, closer. Until they all tumbled together on the bed, Ezog's body hot and heavy over Lydia's, as his slick rounded head found her hungry clutching heat. Settling itself close and familiar, seeking itself just a little inside, and...

Lydia shouted as he plunged deep, carving into her with a single swift, staggering stroke. Filling her with him, spreading her wide open around his huge opened orc-cock, as she arched and convulsed against him, needing more, more, *more*.

And yes, there was more, their bodies all driving together now, Tryg's hand still hooked on the red ribbon, while his hips kept slamming, and his hooded, hungry eyes glittered on Ezog's back. On the sight of his own inked name, surely, with Lydia's trembling fingers dragging against it.

"So sweet," Tryg gasped again, between thrusts, as if it were a mantra, or a prayer. "So good, my pretty pets. You shall both be mine for always, ach? You shall be glad"—his eyes flashed, his thrusts punching harder—"to dress for me, to gift each other to me. To wear my ribbons and my jewels deep inside you. To write my name on your skin, and welcome my gold round your pretty necks, and show all who see you that you belong to *me*—"

His voice was rising, breaking, his head tilting back as he plunged in and held—and oh, that was it, that was it. Ezog's body arching stiff and strong between them, drinking up Tryg's seed deep inside him, and spewing out its own hot nectar into Lydia's wildly shuddering heat. Sharp enough that Lydia's own ecstasy flared up bright and furious, too, clamping her again and again around Ezog's fat, sweet, still-spurting invasion. Filling her, consuming her, flooding and fucking her with his scent, his strength, his safety.

When the pleasure finally flickered away again, they were all collapsed and sticky on the bed together, their breaths heaving hard. And Ezog's mouth was already seeking at Lydia's throat, finding its familiar place, and Lydia gasped as she welcomed it, first that sweet pierce of pain, and then the slow, settled peace of it. Of honouring her gift, caring for her gift, while Tryg blinked down at them both with hazy, approving eyes.

"Such a good gift, sweet thing," he breathed, and Lydia could feel his hand joining hers, stroking with her over Ezog's back, over his own inked name. "Couldn't ask for better."

His voice was hushed, almost worshipful, and in Lydia's

boneless, sated state, it was easy, too easy, to smile up toward him, shy and grateful. "We really are still all you want for Yule?" she murmured. "Even years later?"

Tryg's eyes shifted, shining with strange, sudden brightness—but then he blinked at Ezog's back, exhaled heavy and slow. "Ach, you are," he said, quiet. "Don't like to speak of it, but you ken I spent so many of my days lost in war, and in loneliness. Not trusting my own clan, my own kin, my home. But"—his shoulders heaved—"my *elskan*, and now you, sweet thing, you've granted me gifts I never knew could be truth. Not only your pretty bodies and your pleasure, but this—trust. This fealty. This... *knowing*. Being kin, being here, being *mine*. For always."

His voice had gone low and fierce, his eyes glittering on his name on Ezog's back, on that ribbon at Ezog's throat. And Lydia's finger was gently stroking at the ribbon too, as something dipped and shivered, low in her belly. "I'm so glad, Tryg," she whispered back. "You've been such a gift to us, too. And you know we're glad to honour you, however it might please you. Whether it's giving you gifts, or being marked with your name, or"—she swallowed, gave him another shy smile—"or wearing your gold around our necks."

Because she certainly hadn't missed him saying that, there at the end—and she knew Ezog hadn't either, his attention now almost palpable in his body beneath her fingers. And behind Ezog, Tryg's eyes had visibly widened, his tooth biting his lip—but then he shook his head, a little too quick, too dismissive.

"Ach, you've already done enough, sweet thing," he said, in a bright tone that didn't at all match his shifting eyes. "More than enough. Don't need to do another thing, or wear another thing, either."

But at that, Ezog carefully detached his mouth from Lydia's neck, giving it a few careful licks before drawing away, and twisting himself around to look at Tryg. "You ken we should welcome this, Tryg," he said, his voice disarmingly soft. "Should you truly wish to give it."

There was an instant's silence, and Tryg's eyes blinked, glimmered on Ezog's face—but then he swallowed, thick and audible in his throat. "But it's—a Ka-esh custom," he croaked. "Not Skai. Not—mine."

Lydia wasn't fully following, now, but Ezog's eyes stayed steady on Tryg's, his body shifting around and up, so he could clasp at Tryg's shoulder. "Ach, yours, just as we are," he said firmly. "And you now have a Ka-esh son, do you not? And I ken you would have spoken to him of this, and made sure there was naught amiss with it. Ach?"

Lydia was barely breathing, blinking at where Tryg's face had gone strangely uncertain, making him look disarmingly young, almost innocent. "Ach," he said, quiet. "But you are—sure, Ezog."

It was rare that he used Ezog's name, enough that Lydia couldn't recall ever hearing him speak it—but it only seemed to make Ezog's eyes go softer, his mouth drawing into a slow, tender smile. "I am sure, Sigtryggr," he replied, just as quiet. "Now show us, ach? So our sweet woman can think upon this, also?"

Tryg's eyes dropped, his head twitching a curt little nod. And as Lydia watched, her heart skipping in her chest, he strode over to swipe up the sack he'd brought, and fished around inside it. "Didn't even wrap 'em up," he said thickly, his gaze still cast downwards. "Didn't think I'd really—well. Here."

He'd stalked back toward the bed, thrusting out something gold and shining toward them. Or rather, wait—

two large gold rings, one far thicker and heavier than the other.

Ezog's breath shook at the sight, and his hand reaching to take the rings was shaky, too. But his smile on Tryg's face was even fonder than before, and that red flush had again begun creeping up his cheeks.

"Tryg has brought us each a *kraga*," he said to Lydia, as he passed the smaller, slimmer ring into her hand. "Just like the one our son has given his mate, ach?"

Oh. Ohhhhh. The vision of Eben's *kraga* instantly swarmed through Lydia's thoughts, but yes, yes, of course, these were the same. The circle of solid, gleaming gold, with beautiful script engraving all around the inside, and a clever little latch, opposite a seamless-looking hinge. Meant to snap close around a wearer's neck, and make a perfect fit. And Lydia could still recall Eben's starry eyes as he'd stroked his own *kraga*, and softly told her that the latch couldn't be undone, now that Tryggr had fastened it. And unless a *kraga* was melted, or broken, it would forever be worn as an irrevocable proof of the bond between mates. Not only throughout this life, but into death, and beyond.

"Just liked the look of it, on m'boy's own pet," Tryg said, speaking too quickly, his rather wild eyes darting between Ezog and Lydia. "Thought they'd be fun to play with—with ribbons and chains and the like, you ken. An' they have my vows to you carved on the inside, too. But there's no need, it's not a Skai custom, yund I ken it's a lot to ask, so—"

He looked nearly ready to snatch the *kragas* back again, his lean body gone so taut it was quivering, his eyes darting almost panicked between Lydia and Ezog. And Lydia was deeply, thoroughly grateful when Ezog firmly grasped Tryg's hand, and placed his *kraga* within it.

"I should be most honoured to wear your *kraga*, Tryg," he said softly. "It should be a great, great gift toward me."

Tryg's shoulders heavily sagged, his eyes shimmering with affection, with gratefulness—but then he winced, and glanced sideways toward Lydia. "But I wouldn't wish *you* to feel bound upon this, sweet thing," he said, rushed. "It's one thing for my *elskan*, he knows what he's in for by now, but you—"

He didn't finish, his mouth dropping open, because Lydia had thrust her *kraga* back into his hand, too. "I'd be honoured too, Tryg," she said, and she couldn't stop her voice from wavering, the heat already prickling behind her eyes. "We're yours, for always. And getting to wear such a meaningful sign of your loyalty, and your care, it would be—"

She couldn't even finish, flapping her hands at her wet eyes, and without at all meaning to, she threw herself toward him, buried her face in his chest. "It would be—so good of you, Tryg," she choked, into his warm skin. "Such a gift."

She could feel Tryg's familiar body relaxing against her, his breath rustling at her hair, and he slid his arms around her, drew her closer. "Ach?" he said, muffled, into her hair. "You're sure, sweet thing?"

Lydia fervently nodded against him, and oh, now Ezog was here too, his strong arms circling around them both. And it was the best, most wondrous feeling, wrapped so warm and safe between her kind, fierce, generous mates, who'd given her such great, beautiful gifts.

"Who first, then," Tryg finally said, and the lightness was back in his voice, in his eager claws drumming against Lydia's shoulder. "You, *elskan*?"

Lydia and Ezog both nodded at once—gods, Lydia

wanted to see this—and she was already shifting back and around behind Ezog, drawing his long, shining hair away from his strong, scarred neck. So Tryg could settle in front of him on the bed, his hand gently pulling at the red ribbon still encircling Ezog's neck, finally pulling it off and away. And then Tryg snapped the *kraga* open, and brought its thick, rounded gold edge up to Ezog's throat, just where the ribbon had been.

"Still sure, *elskan*?" Tryg murmured, husky, as he carefully closed the kraga around Ezog's neck. "Feels all right?"

The gold looked to be a perfect fit, close but not constricting, and Ezog tilted his head back and forth, tensing the muscles in his neck. "Ach," he said, his eyes fluttering on Tryg's face. "This feels good."

Tryg's smile was swift, relieved, and perhaps a little weepy, too—and with a firm twitch of his fingers, the latch clicked shut. And when Tryg drew away, the *kraga* was now circled close around Ezog's scarred throat, its gold a gleaming, lovely contrast against his deep green skin.

"So pretty," Tryg croaked, dashing a hand at his eye, and in a jerky movement he lurched forward, thrusting his face into Ezog's neck. "Thank you, *elskan*. You—honour me."

Ezog was softly smiling, his hands firmly stroking up and down Tryg's back, even as a streak of wetness slipped down his scarred cheek. "You honour me also," he whispered back, hushed. "Just as you always have, ach?"

Tryg waved it away with a shaky hand, but when he drew back from Ezog again, he still looked decidedly overcome, his eyes blinking hard. But he was smiling, too, warm and wavering, his hand reverently stroking the gold at Ezog's throat.

"So pretty," he said again, a little steadier this time, and oh, that was a twitch of familiar hunger flickering through his eyes. And then flashing higher, hotter, as he glanced at Lydia, his hooded gaze fixed to her still-bare throat.

"An' you're still sure, sweet thing?" he murmured. "You're sure you want to always wear this, for me?"

But Lydia was sure, so sure, so deep it ached. She trusted Tryg, she adored Tryg, she wanted to spend all the rest of her days with Tryg. All of her Yules, for always.

"I'm sure, Tryg," she said, holding his eyes. "I promise."

Tryg was blinking again, giving her another weepy smile—and now it was Ezog settling behind her, drawing her hair back, baring her neck for the *kraga*. So Tryg could bring up the curved gold edge, settle its cool smoothness against her skin. And then he drew the other side closed, circling it around her neck—but again, it wasn't too tight, or too constricting. Just—*there*, strong and steady and safe, just like him.

So Lydia smiled, nodded, waited—and then shivered all over at the strange, stunning sensation of the *kraga* snapping shut. Marking her, claiming her, making her his. Theirs. Forever.

Behind her, Ezog hissed a low groan, his face nudging into her neck, and oh, the way Tryg watched it, his eyes glimmering between them with fierce, sudden triumph. As if he'd gained a great victory, or the ultimate gift—and as Ezog's teeth scraped against Lydia's gold-circled throat, it distantly occurred to Lydia that once again, Tryg had turned it all around. And in the wake of their gift to him, he'd given them such deep, meaningful gifts in return—but gifts that brought him peace, too. Gifts that were also meant for... himself.

And Lydia should have known that, remembered that, trusted that—and going forward, she would. She knew exactly what her sly, stunning mate wanted for Yule, and she would offer it up to him year after year, wrapped in gleaming gold jewels and silken red ribbons. For all the Yules they had left.

"So pretty, my sweets," Tryg said again, with such fond, tender, hungry light in his eyes. "Now, mayhap we ought to bring back those ribbons, you ken? Leash my sweet pets nice and close, so you'll never escape from me again, ach?"

And Lydia could only smile at him, and throw herself back into his waiting arms, while Ezog's warm strength folded around them both. "Ach," she said, merry and light, as the peace shone and sparkled in her heart. "Let's get the ribbons."

THE END

THANKS FOR READING!

Thank you so much for joining me for this spicy Yuletide tale! I did NOT expect to get as invested as I did in this one... it was supposed to be just a silly little holiday drabble, but then Sigtryggr showed up with his devious plans, and it all went downhill (uphill?) from there! I really hope you had as much fun with it as I did.

I do need to credit my awesome readers on Discord for sparking the entire idea in the first place! We have a lot of fun discussions about characters, and one question that's come up multiple times is whether we'll ever see a MMF with Tryggr and Eben, who we first meet in *The Maid and the Orcs*. I've hated to keep saying that I'm not sure I see it for them... BUT... I could totally see Tryggr's sexy silver fox Pa going for it with gusto! So off this story went. :)

This was also my first time writing a book with main characters who are beyond their 20s and 30s, and it was honestly so refreshing! Thank you to all of you who requested this, and I really hope it worked for you (though I welcome feedback too). I do feel very strongly that more diversity in Romance is awesome for all of us, and that definitely extends to character ages as well.

This was also my first time posting a story early on Patreon, and I'm so, so thankful to each and every one of my patrons for coming on board, and so generously supporting my writing. It's been such a joy sharing this journey with you!

Also, I want to thank all my generous beta readers who were SO flexible with reading and sharing feedback on my unexpected holiday project. Many, many thanks to Amy F., Ari, Cookie, Erin, Jane Mwaniki, Jen R., Judi S., Karen Meeus, Lauren Mauchley, Rowan Phillips, Serena, and V.C. Lancaster (whose books are fantastic, if you haven't read them already!). And special thanks to the fabulous Kahaula, and also to my brilliant second brain MK (who has always been an Ezog cheerleader from the start!).

I also want to extend my deepest gratitude to Goddess Ruby Dixon and Genius Eris Adderly; to MK, Amy, and Elizabeth for helping to keep my Discord a safe and supportive place so we can have all the fun conversations; to Katie (aka Romantically Inclined) for the daily laughs on Instagram; to our gifted Grisk galdr-spinner Morning Dove for all the tales and support; and to Erin for her incredible artwork and continued leadership of the Skai Mafia PR Team! AND, a huge thank-you to Chloe, Coco, and Serene Yoshiko for creating such awesome character art from this book (and so much more) to share with us. You can find it all on my website and social media channels, OR get the full spicy versions on my Patreon!

Finally, as always, I need to thank my own sexy, unbelievably supportive Skai orc, who I plan to keep for all the Yules I have left, too.

I hope you have the loveliest Yule! Hugs and happy holidays!

TRYGGRED BY THE ORC

He's supposed to run... but he wants to be caught.

In a world of orcs and men, Eben of Clan Ka-esh is shy, awkward, and desperately lonely. No one notices the sickroom's quietest scholar, not even when he's saving lives, or offering up decadent pleasures in Orc Mountain's darkest depths.

Until Tryggr, of Clan Skai. A tall, shameless, laughing orc warrior, who can have anyone he wants...

And Tryggr keeps looking at Eben. *Seeing* Eben.

But Skai are risky, reckless, dangerous—and all his life, Eben's been taught to run from them. To hide safe and quiet and alone. Unless he wants to be trapped, crushed, forever marked and conquered beneath a deadly Skai's claws and teeth...

But maybe Eben *wants* to be conquered.

And maybe Tryggr is just the conqueror he needs...

ALSO BY FINLEY FENN

THE LADY AND THE ORC

He's the most feared monster in the realm. And she's what he needs to win his war...

In a world of warring orcs and men, Lady Norr is condemned to a childless marriage, a cruel lord husband, and a life of genteel poverty—until the day her home is ransacked by a horde. And leading the charge is their hulking, deadly orc captain: the infamous Grimarr.

And Grimarr has a wicked plan for Lady Norr, and for ending this war once and for all. She's going to become his captive—and the perfect snare for Lord Norr.

There's no possible escape, and soon Lady Norr is dragged off toward Orc Mountain in the powerful arms of her greatest enemy. A ruthless, commanding warlord, with a velvet voice and mouthwatering scent, who awakens every forbidden hunger she never knew she had...

But Grimarr refuses to accept half measures—in war, or in pleasure. And before he'll conquer Lady Norr's deepest, darkest desires, she needs to surrender *everything*.

Her allegiance.

Her wedding ring.

Her future...

And with her husband's forces giving chase, Lady Norr can't afford to play such a dangerous game—or can she? **Even if this deadly orc's plans might be the only way to save them all?**

ABOUT THE AUTHOR

Finley Fenn is "the queen of dark orc romance" (Virgo Reader), and her ongoing Orc Sworn series has been praised as "sexy, romantic, angsty, and captivating ... utter brilliance" (Romantically Inclined Reviews).

When she's not obsessing over her stories, Finley loves reading, drooling over delicious orc artwork, and spending time with her incredible readers on Patreon, Discord, and Facebook. She lives in Canada with her beloved family, including her very own grumpy, gorgeous orc husband.

For free bonus stories and epilogues, special offers, and exclusive Orc Sworn artwork, sign up at finleyfenn.com.